Children & Lovers

Fifteen Stories

Children & Lovers

by Helga Sandburg

Harcourt Brace Jovanovich / New York and London

Some of these stories appeared originally in *Georgia Review,
Redbook, Seventeen,* and *The Virginia Quarterly Review.* "Blue
Neckerchief," © 1959 by Abbott Laboratories, originally appeared in
What's New, December 1959, and is reprinted with the permission
of Abbott Laboratories.

Library of Congress Cataloging in Publication Data

Sandburg, Helga.
Children & lovers.

CONTENTS: The innocent.—Ah, love.—The grandmother. [etc.]
I. Title.
PZ4.S1933Ch   [PS3569.A48]   813'.5'4   75–42207
ISBN 0–15–117250–1

First edition

B C D E

For
Paula, John and Douglas

Contents

Children & Lovers

The Innocent

Wolfe was big for nine and he swung his fists, practiced, at the
two older girls. They clung together, giggling, shoulders turned
to receive his blows. Autumn had come to the village of Beech
Tree, Michigan, and with it the opening of school. The balmy
wind flung itself down the street so that the tin sign hanging
outside the meat market creaked. Under it Wolfe was yelling,
"Leave my sister alone!"

His taunters sprinted away:

> *"Policeman, policeman, can't you see?*
> *Wolfe Koenig is killing me!"*

"All you do is fight, fight," Fritzi told her brother dispassion-
ately. "Pa said not to."

Wolfe ran his arm across his face in a defiant gesture. His red-
brown hair stood up like a broom. He picked up his workman's
lunch bucket from where he had pitched it onto the pavement
five minutes before. He shook it experimentally, recognizing the
sound of broken glass in the thermos bottle. He sighed and
followed his sister down the street.

They had a mile to walk to the farm outside Beech Tree. The
family had just moved there from northern Indiana; the lease
was signed. Their parents, who had emigrated from Luxembourg after the war, were country people, and accustomed to
animals and soil and harvests. In the way of those who had
survived invasion of their country, they were conscious of the

3

patriotism they felt for their adopted land. But they were unable to forget the invasion; for one thing, Paul Koenig had a dent in the bones of his forehead below the hairline. He was apt to rub it when upset.

"I like autumn. I like this time of year," Fritzi declared. She waited for Wolfe to catch up. Two years older, she was a full head taller—slim, olive-skinned, her black, silky hair short under the beret she wore. "How about you? Is this your favorite time of year?"

He nodded, looking up at her in the pale late-afternoon sun. "Don't tell that I hit those girls, Fritzi."

She smiled. "Why?"

"Just don't tell."

"But I've got to have a reason."

"Just don't, when I say not to."

"People should tell the truth. That's what everyone says." Fritzi liked people. She pulled a piece of sweetgrass as she walked; she sucked it.

"And don't tell why, either."

"I don't even know why. Who knows?" She offered her brother a stem of the grass.

He accepted it, thinking in a flooding of love for her and wrath for her attackers that he could spend his life in his sister's defense. "When we're big, you can keep house for me, Fritzi."

"I wish I had some popcorn right now. Don't you?"

He frowned and fingered his khaki shirt pocket where the note to Mama from the teacher lay. But when they reached the farm gate there was such confusion he forgot all about it. His father, tall and heavy, was in a fury, his reddish beard thrusting from his jaw, his blue eyes on fire.

"They've broke through the fence and gone off somewhere!"

His wife came running from the house. "What's wrong, Pa?" Anna Koenig's face was flushed, her glasses steamy, from the canning going on in her kitchen.

"It's the sows now!" There were a dozen brood Yorkshires, long-legged, white, bred for bacon, not lard. Their offspring was a certain money crop for Paul Koenig's family. Most of the old ones weighed over half a ton each. Paul had showed the pick of them in the ring at the Indiana State Fair, and as a result had a pasteboard box of ribbons, and a Governor's Cup that stood on the parlor table.

"Well, have you hunted for them?"

"What you think, Anna!" He saw the children and spoke more mildly. "You kids come on and help me track them down."

"I got the timer set," the woman worried. "Should I come too?"

But the man and children were already moving away. She let them go, picking up the lunch pails—a little woman, her hair gray early, her body strong. In the house at the sink, she discovered the shattered glass. "Fritzi. That child of mine. Always breaking things." Anna never quite acknowledged that her daughter's mind was slow to grow, and her body had long since outpaced it. She kept the thought away and set up a barrier against it.

There had been an innocent in the village in Luxembourg beside the farms where she and Paul Koenig grew up. In the first week of the Nazi invasion he was shot, having disobeyed and crossed a forbidden bridge. He had not understood the order and had gone over to hawk his May flowers. A group of villagers had marched across the bridge to his body, and the Germans had put them in jail, then sent some of them down the road to Liège and on to a prison camp. They had beat Paul, who was only fifteen but already as big as a man, and scrappy.

Anna, taking a towel, lifted the nine bright half-gallon jars of tomatoes out of the boiling water and tightened the lids. She felt the strangeness of her new kitchen, and the loneliness of not yet knowing her neighbors. She sensed the trouble, the ill feelings, that could result from the strong-headed mother pigs, most of them pregnant, rooting and scavenging on another's land. In her emotion she jerked her hand so that she splashed the hot water and had to smear fat on her arm. She stood quietly looking out the window, rubbing the skin surface, speaking to the cat asleep on the sill.

"And it's a shame, too, that kids have to grow up. There's both of them already in the same grade this year. I don't like it. Both of them in the fourth grade together."

Less than an hour later, Wolfe and Fritzi came tramping in, boisterous, shoving, laughing, so Anna knew the sows had been driven home again. "Where were they? Hey!"

"Say, Mama, it was our Fritzi said to go on up the road."

"Did they get into somebody's field?" Anxious, she put her hand on Wolfe's shoulder.

"No, they were just crowding up the roadway. Pa thought they were in the woods. But Fritzi was right."

"I have to have money for books." Fritzi pulled off her beret and threw it on a chair.

The mother was pleased. "You do have a way. Hasn't she, Wolfe?"

"Everyone has to get their schoolbooks right away," the girl insisted.

"Well, then," said Anna, "you know who to ask. Go hang up your cap."

"But the teacher gave a list to everybody except me," Fritzi cried. "Did she give you a list for me, Wolfe?"

They turned to the boy, who was picking up the cat from the window sill, his back to them. "I've got a note from Miss Freeman about Fritzi."

Anna stood at the sink, looking at him, poised. "Who's she?"

"Teacher," Fritzi said.

"My hands are wet. What's she want, then? Can't she stick to teaching?"

"Oh, Mama," Wolfe said.

"Well, put the note on the table. And Fritzi, take your cap and do like I said."

"I want to open the door for Pa," the girl called. "Wolfe, here comes Pa!"

But Wolfe would not race with her tonight. He felt his mother's thoughts turning: he expected a row. He stated to the windowpane, "Don't I hate school!" And pushed the cat away.

Paul Koenig came in with a pail of yellowish milk, tainted from a strong fall weed the two cows had got into. "Bet this milk is off, Mama." He went to the sink to wash. "Looks like a rain coming."

"You do what I said or I'm going to spank, Fritzi!" Anna cried.

Wolfe already had the beret and was hanging it on the hall hook. "I've got a new joke. Who wants to hear my new joke?"

"There's a note on the table, Paul, from some teacher. Some Miss Freeman." Anna clattered the silverware in a heap onto the table. "Set these out, Wolfe. I haven't had the time to read it."

"So?" Paul eased himself into a chair, leaning his bearded face on his hand. He opened the sheet of paper. He reached a finger to stroke the indentation on his forehead. "Now, this isn't so bad. Fritzi, how'd you like to stay in the third grade another year?"

"She's already passed," Anna said. "In Indiana."

"I liked the first the best," Fritzi said. "I liked being a tree." She spread her arms. "We always were being trees. Did your teacher make you be trees in first, Wolfe?"

Wolfe stood at the table, arranging the silverware at the four places. "Here's the joke. Silence, now." He gave each utensil an extra slap as he placed it.

"Be still," Paul said. "Answer me, Fritzi. Do you mind?"

"I don't even know where the third-grade room is," Fritzi told him.

"I'll find it for you," Wolfe said. "I'll take you there. Hey, listen—there's this French dog meets this American dog on a boat." The boy's auburn hair was mussed; his broad face wrinkled in a grin.

"Don't shout so, then, Wolfe." Anna sighed.

"Be still, Wolfe," Paul said.

"I've got a song today from the boys at recess," Fritzi said.

"No, listen," Wolfe said. "The French dog says, 'My name's Fifi.' *F-i-f-i!* And the American dog says—"

"Will you hold your voice down!" Paul shouted. "Doesn't anybody listen to me?" He caught his wife's angry eyes. The adults gazed at each other, both wearied from the day's round, wanting to avoid argument. The woman turned her glance away stubbornly. She cleaned her glasses on the dish towel.

"How does it look to people, Paul?"

"What is so, is so," Paul said. "You can't hide it like you keep trying to do."

"Sit and eat," said the woman. She passed the serving bowls.

"And this other dog says, this American dog, 'And I'm Fido.' *P-h-y-d-e-a-u-x!* Get it?"

"My father'd have blistered me," Paul said. "All this noise at his supper table."

Fritzi sang out:

> *"One-two-three-four,*
> *Fritzi's Pa went to war;*
> *Four-three-two-one,*
> *Send her back where she came from!"*

"Damn it," Paul said, "this is a madhouse."

"She's a baby," Anna stated. "She's only eleven, Paul."

"Next you'll say kids are kids." He leaned over his plate. He glared at his daughter. "Now, don't they know you're born in America?"

"What, Pa?"

"Forget it!"

"And I don't mind going to the third grade," said Fritzi, "because I don't know any of the kids in fourth yet anyway."

"Who decides whether somebody has to be put back a grade or not?" Anna asked in a frozen voice.

"You asking me, Mama?" Wolfe said. "We took a test."

"And that's that," Paul said. "You satisfied, Mama? Now pass the butter, please. Let's drop the subject."

Wolfe handed over the plate thoughtfully, wondering who the boys were who'd sung at Fritzi and if he'd met them, feeling his profound loyalty. He was relieved, in a way, as well, that his sister would not be in the classroom with him. She tried his patience. He was wondering how he had done on Miss Freeman's test. It had seemed too easy at the time.

"I got in a fight today," he said, without knowing he was going to.

"You're not to do that." His mother's voice was dry, her mouth set. "What grade did Fritzi get?"

"They were teasing her," Wolfe said, ingratiating, "saying, 'Slow poke.'"

"What grade?" Anna said. "I don't want to hear about that."

"She got an F, Anna," Paul said. "It's in the note." He looked at his son. "Were you fighting the same boys who taught Fritzi the song?"

"No. These were a couple of dumb six-grade girls."

"And all Wolfe ever does is fight, fight," Fritzi offered. "And he broke his thermos bottle, too. He threw the lunch bucket!" She laughed.

"Yeah." Wolfe was beginning to laugh too, under his breath, remembering the joy of pitching the bucket onto the cement and flailing at the girls till they ran.

"I'm not going to get you another," Anna said. "You'll have to drink warm milk, then."

"Mama," Paul said, "what's the matter?"

The children were kicking at each other under the table, an edge of hysteria in their giggles. In a sudden movement Fritzi upset her glass of milk and at once began to sob. The room was still except for the sound, as Wolfe hushed his voice, dismayed.

The Innocent

The parents avoided each other's eyes, still bent on their separate arguments that had been laid above the children's chatter. Anna shoved her chair back and went to get a dishcloth. She coaxed, "Here, mop it up. Then you'll feel better."

"No!" Fritzi would not look at her mother; her fists were pounding the table.

"Fritzi," Paul pleaded, "stop that."

"But I spilled it. You can see! I did!" Fritzi's face was contorted. Outside, the wind swung down upon the house, fluttering all of a sudden upon the panes.

"Nobody minds a little milk." Paul stumbled to his feet. "Nobody minds. It's easy to clean up. Can't you understand? This is ridiculous. Now, stop it!"

She looked up at his roaring face, his jutting beard. With a small wail she put her head upon her arms. But the sound seemed made up, artificial.

"I think she's pretending," Paul declared. He built his anger upon his daughter's unreasoned weeping and his own frustration. "All she does is pretend!"

"Pa," Anna cried, "don't dare say that!" She bent over Fritzi.

Paul kicked the chair out of his way. "You spoil her. She's a dummy. Face it! And I take the blame. I think she's my fault, Anna! I've always thought it!" He stomped from the room. The wind rushed in from the porch. The door slammed, violent.

Fritzi lifted her head, ceasing her sobs in the stillness. "I don't want to mop up the milk."

Anna nodded. "Then go to bed. You too, Wolfe."

The children bumped against each other, playing, half-scrambling on the bare stairs. "I'll show you the third-grade room," said Wolfe.

The girl's sweet, high voice came in a half-complaint. "Why did you tell about the fight when you said not to tell? Why, Wolfe? Why!"

Anna Koenig spoke to the cat. "I don't know whose fault

anything is." The rain began to fall softly outside where her husband walked out his old dismay, up and down the yard.

The next day the rain continued, steady, wetting the colored leaves, dissolving old fallen ones, preparing for the first winter freeze. The wind was growing cold and people forgot that only the day before it had blown sweet as one in April. Wolfe and Fritzi prepared their lunches because Anna was so busy. She had two bushels of cucumbers, the last stripped from the dried vines, and was starting pickles, boiling brine for the enormous crocks in the corner. The children made banana-and-peanut-butter sandwiches and wrapped them in brown butcher's paper. They put in bunches of fragrant, dead-ripe Concord grapes. Wolfe filled a pint jar with the pungent, weed-tainted milk.

"Who cares if I have to drink it warm?" he said. "I like it that way."

But at noon he wrinkled his nose and poured it out on the ground. "Ugh." They sat on the stone steps outside the school back door with other farmer children, all of their homes too far to go to for lunch. Wolfe aimed and blew the skins of his grapes at the others. Before long a grapeskin fight developed. Fritzi stayed out of it, her eyes, passive, following her brother.

Wolfe was jubilant, uncontained. He had another note from Miss Freeman. He had unfolded it down in the basement Boys' Room: *Dear Mr. and Mrs. Koenig: Congratulations on a very exceptional child. I spoke to the principal about it and we want you to know that your son Wolfe is being passed into the fifth grade. His score was exceptional: a perfect 100. We feel he would be wasting his time with the fourth class. How proud you must be! Sincerely, Miss Freeman.*

Wolfe nagged, "Hurry up, Fritzi," all the way home. She strolled off to the barn, but Wolfe ran to the kitchen. His mother stood at the sink peeling onions, holding them under water so she would not weep. He slapped the note on the table.

"Hi, Mama." He stood cockily, holding his books to him. "I've got a lot of assignments to do."

She glanced hastily at the small figure. "What's it about, then?"

"Here's another note from the teacher." He almost shouted.

"What's she want now? Why doesn't she just teach?"

"Mama!"

"What's got into you?" Anna was wary.

"I'm promoted to the fifth!"

"What do you mean? Who says?"

"It's here in the letter." He waited, his triumph total.

She sucked a cut on her finger. "We'll see what Pa says."

He was puzzled. "Why?"

"Maybe it's not so good, though. Maybe you ought to learn everything careful as you go along, Wolfe."

"Nobody else got moved up! I want to." He heard the fear that sounded in his tone. "Mama!"

"We'll see what Pa says."

"I guess I know what Pa will say." He tried to hurt her, not comprehending her objection. "He's not mean like you."

But she avoided his look. "Can't you see I'm busy? Supper'll be late. Where's your sister?"

He held his lower lip in his teeth, fingering the piece of paper, once thrilling.

"You ought to look out. What kind of a brother do you think you are?"

He felt the injustice and attacked it. "You're a crosspatch, Mama."

"I'm not cross. I just don't like children badgering, then."

"Crosspatch. Sit by the fire and spin." He left his books on the table, the tears within him pushing up. He kicked the door shut and heard his mother's faint protest from the kitchen. He was examining the knowledge that because of Fritzi he would not be allowed to pass to the fifth grade.

She was approaching, crossing the barnyard to him, a basket

clutched against her coat front. She called, "Aren't they cute, Wolfe? I get to feed them. They're mine."

Their father appeared at the barn door, grinning, a pitchfork in his hands. "Wasn't for your sister, the old one would have eaten them!"

Fritzi hurried to Wolfe. "Look." The dozen pink infant pigs mewed and turned, nuzzling each other. "I got a stick and I made that sow stay back. And I gave all the babies to Pa. Look, will you!"

Wolfe's mouth twitched. "They'll all die."

"No. I'm going to feed them!"

"Doesn't matter. They're sure to die. I hope they do. I hope they turn cold and stiff and die."

"Aren't they cute?" Fritzi was untouched, and adjusted the gunny sack that half-covered the young.

Wolfe spoke, vicious, undertoned. "And you're the biggest, dumbest snot that ever was."

But she was already down the path to the kitchen. "Mama! Open up. Wait till you see!" Her voice was powerful. "I saved them. They're all mine. Pa said!"

Wolfe wandered behind one of the farm buildings and sat on the damp ground. Slowly twilight came and then Fritzi's holler: "Supper! Supper, Wolfe!"

He went to the house, and mounting the porch stairs, heard the voices inside the kitchen, his mother saying, "It's too big a difference, two grades apart. It looks queer. Pretty soon he won't even want to play with Fritzi."

"Think of the boy. He's bright. You can't let one of your children stand in the way of the other."

"What does that teacher know? School's school. What's the difference what you learn?" Her voice was shrill, and in the end she won.

Wolfe felt her victory though he had not heard his father's assent. He hung his coat in the hall. When they sat at the table, Paul said that Wolfe was to remain in the fourth. He would write Miss Freeman a letter that Wolfe would give her. "Okay," the boy said. And suddenly when he looked at his sister, he felt the overwhelming quality of his hate. The sensation was so strong that his food repelled him.

"Clean your plate, then," Anna said. "And I made you up a good dessert."

"Who wants dessert?" he mourned, surly.

"Apple cobbler." She wooed him, "I'll whip you some cream if you want."

"The milk stinks this week," Wolfe said. "I poured mine out on the ground at lunch recess."

"He did, too," Fritzi said. "And then they had a grapeskin fight."

"Just you be sure to tell everything." Wolfe swung his legs under the table, feeling his wildness. "Go on!"

"That's enough, now," Paul warned. "Settle down. I was feeling pretty good about saving that lot of pigs."

Wolfe turned the food on his plate. "Fritzi?"

"What?"

"You get any more songs at recess today from those boys?" He felt kin to her tormentors. He approved of them; he wanted to be one too.

"I forgot," Fritzi said. "They gave me a present!"

"The same boys?" Paul asked.

"Where is it?" Wolfe said.

"Run get it," Anna told her daughter. "What is it? Let's see it."

"I have to remember where I put it, first," Fritzi said. "It's in my coat pocket or else my room. It's bound to be somewhere. Who knows?"

"What a double-dyed dummy you are," Wolfe said fiercely to the plate of food before him. He felt his alienation from the sibling who was different, who for the first time caused him true harm. A tragic premonition seeped in, of his future. He saw himself in a house of his own; Fritzi, tall and old, was crumbing it up for him, witless. "I wish I never had you for a sister. I wish!"

"Take that back." Paul rose. "At once!"

But the boy could not stop. He was staring at the tablecloth, avoiding the figure towering. "It is what I wish." His words poured almost without volition. "And you can do anything you want to me, Pa." He looked at Paul. "And I'll never help Fritzi out again."

"You are no son of mine!" Paul reached across the dishes and cuffed Wolfe's ear so that he swung against the table. "Be still and take back what you said. I'm waiting."

White, Anna echoed him. "Do as Pa tells you."

"No matter what name anybody calls her," the boy maintained, his face aflame, his eyes wide.

Only Fritzi was unimpressed. "I think I remember. I think I stuck it in my coat pocket, Wolfe."

"I hate you! I hate Fritzi!" Wolfe spoke it in a vast relief.

Fritzi went into the hall as Paul struck his son again. The child of nine and the man of thirty-six measured each other and both knew that Wolfe was due to lose. In the silence they could hear Fritzi whispering to her pigs as she went by the round basket, leaning over to touch their silken skins. Neither Wolfe nor his father moved. "I am waiting on you," Paul said.

Held to each other, they could almost not turn to look when Anna caught her breath, snatching the toy from Fritzi.

"Those bad boys! What are we going to do, Paul?"

It was a tiny dime-store toilet with a hinged seat. Fritzi sang:

> "When Fritzi was a little girl
> They fed her castor oil,
> And every time that she sat down
> She fertilized the soil!"

She reached out and took her gift back from her mother. With soft fingers she moved the seat up and down. "It really works. And I love it."

Paul sank back, his temper turned, leaning his bearded chin

on a hand. He whispered, "You love your friends, Fritzi, who teach you verses. Don't you?" His face was tired.

"I think it's disgusting, then!" Anna was riled and she got up. "Downright. And I don't want everyone talking about it, either." She was clearing the dishes, bringing the apple pie.

"And I can say what a girl wrote down in an autograph book too, Wolfe," Fritzi said. "And when I can write good, I'll write it for you."

Wolfe leaned back in his chair, starting to giggle. "*I wish you health, I wish you wealth.*" Is that it?"

"No. It's:

> "*When you get married*
> *And live in a tree*
> *Send me a coconut C.O.D.!*"

"Oh, Fritzi." Wolfe's blue eyes, brilliant like Paul's, stayed with his sister's brown ones. "I think I'm getting the giggles!"

"Me too." She joined his muted laughter, unresisting. He squealed:

> "*I wish you health,*
> *I wish you wealth,*
> *I wish you friends galore.*
> *I wish you heaven after death,*
> *Who could wish for more!*"

They put their hands over their mouths.

"Oh, I'm dying, Wolfe!"

"Stop, Fritzi."

Outside, the rain had quit, and the moon, lavender and heavy, came up newly from the earth. Anna was spooning the cobbler into bowls, sober, half-indulgent. "Such nonsense. It's bedtime, then."

"Finish up. Go along," Paul told them. "And take that thing with you, Fritzi."

When they had shut the stairway door, Paul rubbed his forehead scar. His mind dwelled on the countryside in Luxembourg where, for the sake of an innocent like his daughter, the courage of a score of men had blazed up.

Anna rattled the plates, pressing him. "You're going to let him, aren't you?"

"What?"

"Go on to the fifth. I can tell you are. No use to talk."

He nodded. "Miss Freeman even took it up with the principal. Now, that shows she thought it was important."

"I supposed you would in the end anyway." Anna wished that time would wait a while. She kept needing more of it over the presaging years, to understand.

The thoughts of the couple, unarticulated, hung like weighted, unrung bells in the room.

Ah, Love

Bliss woke with a sensation of peace that she couldn't explain. She lay listening to the occasional rush of one of the heavy trucks that ran down the street below the rooming-house window. She stared at the wallpaper where a small stain clung to the rose trellis design like a honeybee; she could almost hear it humming. Love, she thought. Dan. That was it; he'd called last night. Today was to be their day. And it was past due. Savoring her body's peace, she tried to summon his image. But she could only recall that he was tall and quick-tempered and told little jokes. She put his words into the air and tried to hear him say them, "My patter, does it amuse you, Bliss?" She couldn't remember one joke he'd ever told. But his lips pursed when he laughed, the mouth drawn in a little smile. Ah, love!

She got out of bed, glancing at the clock. She ran to the window; the last of the sunrise was glowing.

> *Red sky at dawning, Travelers take warning;*
> *Red sky at night, Travelers delight.*

Bliss didn't believe it. The day would be perfect, and God was in His heaven. They would eat their picnic lunch under the bridge by the canal. She could see his smile there in the pale sunlight. It was high time they had a day and a night with each other. It sounded like eternity to Bliss, leaning at the soot-dusted window.

She was twenty this year and knew her own mind. Two years

ago she'd come in from the farm, one of six sisters, to take a job clerking at the bank. After a year, she'd become Mr. Wilson's secretary. She sent home a part of her check every week. Bliss thought of herself as plain; she had yellow hair, was tall and slim, her breasts high. She walked in the elastic stride of country people. The first time they'd met, Dan and she had left the Wilson party and gone down to the bridge that ran across the pond. Mr. Wilson was Chairman of the Board at the bank. Dan had said, "What a way you have of walking, Bliss!" His voice thick and hurried from having to say so much to her in such a short while.

Bliss had never been in love before. It was pain mostly, she felt. Unless she was with Dan. She could count on one hand the times they had been alone. Otherwise she saw him under the eyes of townspeople at one of Mr. Wilson's get-togethers, or when she looked up from the desk and saw Dan walk into the bank, over to the cashier's window, his eye roaming briefly again and again to her low-fenced cubicle, afraid his attention would be noted. They had met undisturbed for a quarter or half of an hour at night under the elm trees at the end of the yard of the Public Library. Bliss had suggested the spot, a few blocks from where she roomed. The last time there had been twelve days ago.

Late yesterday evening she'd been in the tiny shower when the telephone bell had pealed. She'd come to stand dripping on the rag rug. He'd said, "Betty's going to visit her mother, Bliss. She's taking the eight o'clock morning train, and she's staying the night. Could you spend tomorrow with me? I'll take off from work. Then I thought we'd go somewhere overnight."

"Yes."

"You don't sound very enthusiastic."

"I am, Dan."

"We'll have all day and all night. We'll drive out to Highgate Inn and park the car and walk along the old canal. It ought to be deserted being the first of the week."

"Yes."

"You tell your boss you're ill. Think Wilson will believe you?" Dan laughed, and then the joyous thing started in Bliss that was here in the morning as she awoke.

"I don't care if he does or not." She'd looked in the mirror over the old wood dresser where the phone stood, and her blue eyes shone. "I look awfully healthy."

"And sweet, the leaves are turning, and it's beautiful in the country. I drove the family out over the weekend, and Highgate Road is glorious." He built the day for her. "We'll walk up to see the falls too. I'll have you all to myself. I'm so greedy for you, Bliss."

"Yes."

"Are you there?"

"Of course."

"You're so quiet."

"What else will we do, Dan?"

"You say that so sweetly. I love your voice. Sometimes I go into the bank when it's not necessary. Beforehand I think about what I'll wear to impress you. I straighten my tie, and I get my shoes polished, and I put on my new flannel coat with the brass buttons. Then I hope you'll go sailing by on your way to Wilson's door, so I can look at you walk. I've never seen a woman swing along like that." His laugh was there. "Then I want to dash after and take you in my arms. Can you picture the consternation that would cause!"

"Dan, shall I pack a lunch?"

"Wonderful. Not too much though. I want you, not food."

"Dan, I like the way you've planned everything."

"What do you expect? I'm the lucky one. Don't think I don't know it. For supper I'll take you to the Inn. We'll have martinis and take hours over the meal. And coffee and brandy afterward. And I'll tell you all the things I ought to be saying all the time to you. What it was like the first time I met you. And what it's been like since. Do you want to hear?"

"Dan."

He heard the love in her voice, "I adore you, Bliss. I want you beside me right now."

And she wanted him, the dark eyes, the fingers in her hair. And her hands at rest on his shirt, feeling the warmth of him and the beating heart. Love was a burden, she felt; how did people endure this pain about their hearts through the long stream of ages? "Dan?"

"What is it, sweet?"

"I'll bring a little cheese and fruit. Will that be all right?"

"You dear! Now pay attention. We'll meet just after nine. You leave your room on the dot and start walking down Pine Street going south. I'll be leaving the garage at the same time, and I'll pick you up. Have you got it?"

"Yes, Dan."

"Good-bye, sweet."

She had stood half-chilled in the lamplight, hearing the water drip on the metal shower floor. A feeling like grace had flowed into her. She'd gone back to turn on the shower and whistle loudly as the water rushed upon her skin.

Now she was at the morning window, breathing the autumn air, almost as warm as summer, somnolent, honey-scented. Bliss had never spent a night with a man; she was ready to give herself to this lover. The coming twenty-four hours were all there was of life, she felt; there was no existence after them. The clock was saying eight; in an hour the happiness would start. At the party where they first met, their hands had touched among the silver at the buffet. Dan had given Bliss the plate he'd filled, and then got one for himself; they'd sat in low chairs in a shadowy corner, not even eating the food, until he said it was stuffy, and they set their plates down and slipped out the terrace door into the night. There a horned thin moon shone, and the path was obscure, and the pond was of silvery metal.

The phone rang out, and Bliss hurried from the window to get it.

Ah, Love

"One of the kids has a cold."

"I knew it, Dan," she whispered.

"What? I can't hear you, Bliss. Anyway, Betty's decided not to stay over with her mother. She'll be home tonight on the nine-forty-two. She's just taken the eight o'clock. I argued but Betty'd think something was wrong if I got too vehement. You start out at ten for Pine Street." His voice was angry.

"I thought you said nine."

"There was some trouble with the sitter. I've got to wait until she gets here. So we'd better say ten." His tone changed. "Sweet? Bliss?"

"I'll leave my room on the hour."

"Good-bye."

She hung up. Her white cotton gown swirled about her as she strode, swift, across the floor. She drew the calico curtains that concealed the kitchen counter and cupboards, the tiny combination stove and refrigerator. She frowned, taking out the piece of Wisconsin cheddar. It was smaller than she'd thought, but would do. She got a chair and rummaged about in the high shelves for a tin of Danish ham she'd bought once. She arranged the basket, putting in white napkins and silver knives and Rambo apples from her father's farm, which she polished. Bliss sniffed their perfume and began to whistle. She had new peach wine from the farm too, and she drew some off into a bottle and put it in. And two tiny glasses. After all, a day was a day, and she had no complaints. They would have a night some other time. She folded a white tablecloth over the top and tucked its edges in.

At the Inn that evening she would ask for lobster or steak prepared in some delicate alien way she'd only read about and never tasted. And Dan would order it for her, whatever she liked, their first dinner alone. All the while, he would be saying his praises of Bliss. She set the basket by the door and went to the closet, knowing what she would wear: the blue dress. There was a black that she'd used to like, but not any more. She smoothed the lacy blue of the sleeves, before laying it out on a chair, ready to slip into.

At eight-thirty, Bliss rang up the bank and talked to a teller who was her friend and sometimes took her to a moving picture. He told her to keep warm and to stay home an extra day if she wanted. She began to get herself ready, filling the time before ten. She dallied over her nails and brushed her hair and mended a tear in her slip; as she went back and forth, her reflection passed in and out of the small mirror. She glanced at the unreal half-dressed figure, the gown behind it a drift of white at the bedside. Who could say if the girl in the mirror was herself or not? Others saw the real Bliss, she only her reversed image in the glass, face plain, lips pale, the long hair blond. She put on lipstick and began to bind up her hair.

When it was done to suit her, it was time to go, and she went to slip on her dress. The phone jingled; she tore the garment off hurriedly. "Yes?"

A business matter had come up; Dan was in real estate. "It's the one piece of property I can't leave to my partner, Bliss. I have to handle it myself; it's important. Sweet, I don't know what to say."

"It's all right, Dan."

"No, it's not. I'm so frustrated. Why these clients today! But, I'm sure I'll be rid of them by noon. We'll plan on one o'clock to be safe. Is that all right?"

"Of course."

"Don't sound so small. We'll have from one until nine tonight. Eight hours, Bliss. We've never had that much. And it's in just a little while."

He had hung up, and she began to walk about; she kicked at the white heap of nightgown, shrugging, thinking she didn't care really. Once Bliss had been redeemed. It had happened out in the country church when she was going on sixteen. The preacher had shouted the hundredth psalm when he'd fought the devil, flooring him with both feet. He'd yelled about fire and domesday, and then coaxed the people with white robes and the kindness of God.

After a week of the meetings, Bliss had felt grace flood into her in a sort of ecstasy. She'd gone up with a whole crowd and got baptised. The Divine influence had lasted almost a year. Ah, love! she had thought. *The Bridegroom comes; open you the gates.* For those months a mysterious beauty, a radiance, infused the commonest chores; getting in the cows, setting the broody hens, mixing the mash for hungry goslings. Then somehow the feeling had waned, and one day she knew it was gone altogether. But she didn't forget how it had been, and how it satisfied a necessity in her.

Bliss tried to think what to do in the lake of time that spread between now and one o'clock. She decided to unpack the lunch basket. She took it by its handle and then up into her arms, holding it tightly. She leaned on the kitchen counter, afraid for a moment she might cry. She left the basket there and closed the calico curtains. She went to the window to look at the fair and unused morning. She could hear the clock's murmur as its hands went round.

They pointed out noon when Bliss rose, her blood beginning to quicken and her weakness to shed. She put on the blue dress, and arranged her hair again, at the mirror. Her hand was quick, as the bell reverberated, echoing against the wood of the dresser. "Dan?"

His words were clipped, cheery. "Hello there, Bob? I can't make that lunch date at one o'clock. Suppose you just go ahead and eat. There's another new client here and we're doing business. We've just sent out for sandwiches and coffee. I feel like that cross-eyed fellow who said, 'May I have this dance?' and both old maids got up and told him, 'Yes!'" He laughed. "I'm awfully sorry, Bob! I'll call up about that other matter we spoke of at around three. Will that be all right?"

"Dan," she told him. "Love and love!"

He seemed to hesitate, and then there was the click. She

looked down at the lacy blue sleeves. At the bridge where they had leaned on the bamboo railing, he had said she must dress in blue always; it was Bliss's color. "On your fair skin, black is wrong. Always wear the color of your eyes!"

Leaves were being raked and burned down the street; the dying odor drifted, nostalgic and powerful. Bliss thought, in a little while you'll be sitting beside Dan, driving out to where the trees are all changed and bright and not their ordinary green selves any more. They'll be glorious. "I drove the family down Highgate Road on the weekend, Bliss. Beautiful." The wife beside, and the children prattling in the back.

At three-fifteen, she was standing at the phone. Her eyes wandered over the wallpaper roses and the rusty spot like an old beetle that refused to fly and clung there. At a quarter to four she dialed his office. His secretary answered, and without a word Bliss replaced the instrument on the cradle. A wind had started up, whining about the old rooming house, rushing through the open window, chill. She listened to the first thunder muttering far away. There was a high jingle of the phone. Bliss leaped to answer.

He was as distant as the storm's warning. "I can't make today at all. I got caught at three and couldn't phone. Did you understand when I spoke to you at noon that there were people here in the office?"

"Yes, I did."

"I hoped you would. Business is business." Dan was a stranger, Bliss felt, as her love drooped and only a pierce of pride kept her tears at bay. "But sweet, we're going to have our dinner together. I'll come in front of your place at six. Be dark by then. You watch for me at the window, and I'll wait half a block down the street. I'll drive slowly and dim the lights, so you'll know it's me."

"All right."

"I can't hear you. Something wrong with this connection!" Abrupt, impatient, his voice retreated, and he spoke to someone there, "Get the hell out until I ring for you." He returned to Bliss. "Don't you ever give your name on this phone. Are you listening?"

"Dan."

"I'm so sorry, sweet." His far-away voice continued, "But I've got a new coat hanging here. And I want you to go put on something just for me, that's sleek and black and sleeveless. Is everything all right? Say it is, now."

"Yes."

"Six o'clock. Good-bye."

She thought, it isn't his forgetting a blue dress. And it isn't his temper. Or his distant tone. Not even his making the love diminish. She stripped off the dress and threw it down. It's the way things are. I don't like God; not a bit. If He is at all! She declared it to wound Him, the final straw being disbelief. She got out the black dress and thought how unbecoming it was. And how little she cared.

Minutes went by quickly because of her new wrath. As dusk began to enclose the buildings across the street, a spate of rain came. It subsided, and with it her anger. Street lights flicked on, and people passed to and fro on the wet pavement below. They were all hurrying to someone, on rendezvous with wives, children, parents, somebody for everyone. None went slowly. None stood quietly at a window but Bliss. Her hand scarcely touched the curtain; the fragrant damp wind fanned her. She was consumed in her waiting and in the doubt that had risen in her that he would not come. They would not meet. The day was over.

The clock said seven as she vacillated and decided that no, she would not call him at his home, even though surely he must be there and would answer. But already she was dialing. Betty's voice was in her ear, distinct, "Hello?"

Bliss stammered, putting a twist into her voice, that she had a wrong number. She moved about in the lamplight as the rain began to beat steadily upon the house, and blow in on her floor.

She hung the black dress in the closet. She hated having changed her mind about her dress because of him. When she began to weep, it wasn't stormily, as when she'd been a child. It was almost noiseless; and it was new to Bliss, and bitter, and had to do with becoming a woman.

Then the bell pealed, vibrating, echoing. She hesitated before going to it. He had been divorced from her thoughts, and she was unprepared. "Bliss! Sweet?"

"This is Bliss."

"Betty's come home."

"Oh."

"I'm over at the drugstore. Look, in a few minutes, about ten, I'll say I'm going for a walk, cigarettes, something. Meet me at our place. Bliss? Be there."

"Yes. All right."

He was gone, and she felt how the day had passed in a moment. All that was necessary now was that she put her hands under his coat and feel the heart throb. It was imperative for her to know that he was real. He was no shadow in a glass. Hasty, she snatched the blue dress from the floor. She gave a quick sweep at her disheveled hair and forgot her lipstick. She ran down the stairs in half a panic, and her light coat was drenched when she reached the Library yard.

He was outlined against the bole of an elm; there was the red coal of his cigarette. She walked up to the figure. He crushed her to him, his mouth caressing lips, eyes, her throat. There was his voice at her ear. "Bliss. Sweet sweet beautiful."

"Ah, love," she told him.

"There'll be another chance," he whispered. "Don't worry. I adore you. Your face is soft in the rain. Why didn't you bring an umbrella? You'll catch a cold." He laughed.

"I'm too healthy!"

"On the phone you sounded angry. When you said, 'This is Bliss,' I didn't even recognize you."

"I can hear your heart." Her palm covered it and she

thought, this moment is forever. God, I'm sorry I blamed You.

"I have to go, Bliss. I'll call you up. You get home and dry yourself off. Get nice and warm. Don't ever let anything happen to you, sweet. I couldn't live without you." He folded her tightly to him. "I'm sorry everything went the way it did today."

"We have this moment."

"And there'll be another time. I promise."

"Yes."

"Go along, now. While I'm watching you. I'll wait until you turn the corner, Bliss."

She waved as she went out of his sight. She went in her long country stride down the street in the steady downpour. She tried to whistle and gave it up. Bliss was comprehending that in the same way that grace had infused her being when she was sixteen, love had arrived at twenty. She would wait until its radiance also waned and was spent.

After a while, she managed to mount the staircase to her silent room where the mirror in the darkness reflected nothing.

The Grandmother

She was watching the boy play tennis, his skinny thirteen-year-old body leaping high, returning the ball with powerful strokes. His white shorts were dirty and his white shirt smudged. Absently she ran her hand over the pet rat Davy, on her shoulder. The boy had promised to play the next set with her. She was devoted to him. Even when they fought and yelled with each other, deep down she was his slave. He knew it, she was sure. She even copied his white sports attire. At nine she was breastless and thought of herself as his twin. "Nice serve," she called. He had a swell overhand.

The sky was dull and hot and milky-white. The sun was testing their endurance; it beat down with a scathing eye of fury, trying their mettle. The two players were panting and the ball thudding on the green, which her father would roll every evening. The court was in good shape this year for the summer people. They would start arriving from the big city in June every year to rent her father's cottages. All day long they would lie on the beach, getting a tan. The boy had been coming ever since she could remember, and they always took the same cottage, *The Robin's Nest*. Her family was alone here in the winter months; they lived in the big house called *The Manse*, surrounded by the rambling cottages. She would walk with her sisters the mile out to Highway 44 and ride the school bus. She would tend her various pets after school. Her three older sisters each had a dog, but when their father offered the girl one, she turned him down and asked for the cavies instead, the guinea pigs. She had four of them in the old doghouse. She had a pair of baby owls, too, that one of the summer people had found and given to her. She fed them ground beef and they would ride tamely on her wrist. And she had two cages full of white rats in the garage, one of males, the other of females. Her father wouldn't let her breed them. Davy was the oldest, the granddaddy. She stroked him and he dozed, his warm bristled nose settling alongside her neck, his hairless pink tail limp.

Then it was game and the boy had won the set. He spun his racket in the air and caught it by the handle as it came down. He swaggered over to the bench where she sat and took the towel she handed him. His father had drilled him on the game and he was a whiz. Her folks couldn't play, but they had bought her a good racket, maybe a little light. She was a natural at the game, the boy had said once. He never remembered when she reminded him of it though.

"Let's go," he said.

"Okay." First she put Davy safe in his box under the bench.

The set score was a dismal one-five, and it was the girl's serve when her eldest sister came driving up in the family car. She struck hard into the ball, showing off. The boy returned it, dropping it just inside the net with a mad spin so she couldn't possibly get it. She faced her sister, seeing her frown. "What's the matter?"

"It's Gran. She's very sick." Her sister nodded in greeting at the boy. "And you have to come home right away and get dressed."

"Why?"

"Gran might be dying. Mother just called. She wants us girls to go and say good-bye to Gran."

"Can we finish this set first?"

"Don't be silly. Quick! You have to change."

"I'm sorry," she said anxiously to the boy.

"That's all right. We'll finish when you get back. You were a little off this morning anyway."

"So long."

"Sorry about your grandmother."

She felt a thrust of excitement at the respect in his voice. She took up Davy's box and followed her sister to the car. Is this grief? she wondered. I don't feel a thing. She tried to remember Gran, whom she had seen a few months ago. There was a vague large figure, dispensing sourballs and arguing with Mother most of the time. She gave it up and got in the car.

Her eldest sister drove all of them to Gran's house thirty miles away. Mother was there; she kissed them, looking worn. She'd been called the night before when Gran first took sick. Absentminded, pale and gentle, Mother moved as though she would shatter if she did something abrupt. And she spoke in a whisper, telling them to sit and wait on the long yielding sofa. The four sisters, crowded into a tight row, sensed the suggestive odor of medicine and deadened agony.

They were soon to be called into the bedroom where the old woman lay. Because the girl was the baby of the family, she sat on the end, next to the eldest, who thought she would be sad and held her hand. The girl examined her mind, probing it. She could feel no sensation unless it was pleasure with the novelty of the happenings. She remembered the tiger cat that had fallen into the cistern last fall and drowned. One of her sisters had said through her tears, "I don't care! I'll get another right away." The girl would do the same if one of her pets died and put her mind at once on the next one.

There was that time her pet rats had gotten too plentiful. She had neglected to divide the sexes the way her father had told her to. The rats had bred all over the place, and it seemed overnight she had about thirty. Her parents said she must get rid of all but six. So she picked out her favorites and put the others in an old bird cage. Her sisters helped. They set the cage in the laundry tub filled with lukewarm water. The rats began to swim and struggle. The girls ran screaming together up the stairs. After half an hour they crept down again. Her heart was crashing like mad because she was so scared. There were the rats, alive, ringed about the edge of the tub, their hides soaked, busily polishing their faces with tiny paws. The scent of wet hair was about them. At first the girl had felt a near resentment at the trick, but then she was elated at their cunning, slipping like snakes, following their pointed noses through the bars. Her father had said she could let them live if she would separate them at once and promise not to let any more have young. So she had two cages now.

Her sister was squeezing her hand as Mother came out. "You may come in now, girls," Mother whispered severely. "Be very quiet. Tiptoe. I don't know if Gran will recognize you."

Gran didn't. She called them by strange names. Elvira and Mabel. Mother gasped, "Those were my sisters! Mabel died years and years ago."

"Be good," Gran's voice mumbled, "when I'm gone."

"Oh, Gran!" Mother turned to her children, a catch in her voice. "You must go home again. I shouldn't have made you come."

"We wanted to," the eldest whispered. "Don't worry."

"She didn't know any of you!" Mother sighed and herded them out.

On the trip home her sisters spoke softly about it. Would Gran truly die? Did it hurt? Gran had looked quite content, propped on the many little pillows. But she hadn't known them. There was a thrill in their voices, talking it over. And then the eldest began to weep, tender. "Gran gave me a string of sugar lumps when I was sixteen. They were tied with red ribbon. Three years ago," she told the girl, "so you wouldn't remember. But Gran said I was sweet sixteen." The tears wet the pretty face.

"I do remember! Yes." The girl thought, I wish I could cry too. From the corner of her eye she watched the drops flow and tried to feel sadness. But there was only a vague envy of her sister. The girl wondered where they would put Gran's dead body. She herself had a private animal graveyard in a grove of spruces. It was one of her secrets that no one knew. When she found a dead bird or if a pet died, she would dig a hole and bury it there, in a handkerchief or a little box lined with cotton batting. She had to push her way through prickly heavy branches to get to the place in the middle of the trees where there were crosses and markers. The first had been her talking crow. She was four at the time and selected the graveyard when she needed a place to put it. The stick had a weatherworn "C" for Crow, since she couldn't write words then. Her father and mother might put a tombstone over Gran if she died. There was a brief moment of fear that Gran might live after all and the excitement would have been for nothing.

At home they made peanut-butter-and-jelly sandwiches and poured glasses of milk. They sat about the screen porch, spilling crumbs that the dogs licked up. The sliding swing creaked; the dogs scuffled and played. The girls were listless and seemed to be waiting. "I'll say one thing," the eldest abruptly declared. "I'm going to stay right here by this phone. I want to know!"

But the girl got up, restless, her small body constrained. "I sure wish it was over."

"You wish Gran was dead?" One of them was being sarcastic to her.

"I didn't mean that. But I can't stand suspense. I can't ever." She stood defiant, to see if there would be a quarrel.

But the sister was coaxing her collie up onto the swing cushions by her. "There's a boy." She tugged its collar. The others, a beagle and a pointer, flopped their tails, hoping to be asked up too.

"I guess I could clean out the cavies' house," the girl said. The boy had probably gone swimming with his folks. He would never in a million come after her for tennis. It was too late in the afternoon.

The Grandmother

"Don't get your dress dirty," the eldest said.

"I won't." The pointer and the beagle followed and at the door she called, "I'm going to lock the screen to keep your dogs in. Don't let them out till I get the cleaning done."

"Okay!" they shouted.

She got a block of straw from the opened bale in the garage, and a scraper and a basket. She went to the old doghouse where they lived. One side was removable, and she unfastened it and laid it on the ground. The four guinea pigs scuttled to the other end; the black male whistled and jiggled his feet. He was darling. She scraped the litter into the basket, the sweat standing on her face, dirt rubbing onto the front of her white flowered skirt. The bottom boards were damp so she decided to let the house air out before she put in the straw. She played with the male and the red young one. She let alone the other two, whose bodies were swollen with young. Their babies were due at any moment! In her opinion one of the greatest things about cavies was that right after birth the young were running about like miniatures. And you never knew how they would turn out. They could be almost any shade, maybe with little spots or splashes or all one solid color like the red one. And they might have up to four babies at a time. They were a very exciting type of pet.

Then she heard his call. The boy! He was standing there at the shaded house door, where her mother had laid out a rock garden. He had called into the house. He looked like a prince, sunburned and tall. He had on fresh-ironed shorts, and a scout knife hung at his belt. She put the pigs down and scrambled to her feet, racing over to him. "Do I have to change my dress?"

"Oh, there you are. How about finishing that set?"

"I thought you went swimming for sure! Should I change?"

"No. Come just like that." He turned and was trotting away, tossing a tennis ball and darting to catch it.

"I'm crazy! Who cares!" Jubilant, she ran after him, snatch-

Children and Lovers

ing her racket from the pathside where she had left it in the morning.

They finished the set, the score an ignominious one-six. She dared him to another and he accepted. They were on the second game, after unbelievably she'd won the first, when barking floated on the air. She didn't heed it. The sun rays were more dogged and desperate than in the early part of the day, having sucked the grass clean of all moisture. The boy and she were perspiring. Her dress was a mess but she didn't care. She ran, smashing the ball. She had a sudden feeling that she might win a set. This might be the time! And then the dogs barked again and she remembered. "Oh, good night!" She dropped her racket at once and wheeled, rushing up the road toward *The Manse*.

"What is it?" he yelled. "Hey!" And was running after her.

"The dogs," she shouted, driving her legs faster up the steep gravelly road. What was that delicious sensation in her body? It couldn't be joy. Was it terror?

He caught up with her, his soft tennis shoes noiseless. "What about them? What's wrong?"

She felt the exquisite rend in her belly, the grind of fear. "I bet they got my guinea pigs. I bet they did!"

"Holy cow!" He padded beside her. "I hope not."

"I just bet they did." She was hopeful, though. She jogged along, feeling the hurt that always came before the second wind. And then they reached her pets' house. It was empty.

The pointer and the collie lay sprawled on the flagstones by the door. They came forward to greet her, panting, heads down, bodies waggling from side to side. They led her to the strewn cavies, nudging them now with indifferent noses. She gathered them one by one in the crook of her arm, soft and dear, their black eyes yet moist. The dogs had killed them instantly, breaking their backs as they did woodchucks and wild rabbits, so except for the saliva there were no marks. The dogs trailed her

---

The Grandmother

around, sheepish, as she was picking them up. The brown-and-white one that had been fattest with young was farthest away of all. She wondered if a dog had dragged it there, or if it had scurried that far, anxious to save itself. Deserted by the girl! In its hour of need, abandoned. Finding it took a long while. The boy was the one who spotted it. He was quiet and helpful and didn't laugh as if he thought she were childish.

She told the dogs to go away. She sat on the flagstones and lined the bodies up before her. From the screen porch on the other side of the house, she could hear her sisters' voices, falling and rising, laughing now and then, in continuous murmur. She gathered her loneliness to her. The bodies were beautiful, the coats shining. "I wonder," she said to the boy standing above her, "where I could get another pair. I have to start looking right away."

He was grave. "It's a shame."

"You don't know anyone who raises them?"

He shook his head. "I know a boy in the city who has rabbits he sells to hospitals."

"I don't care for rabbits." She looked at the wild flowers her mother had planted along the cool flagstones, delicate with gentle colors and fragile ferny leaves. It was almost unbearable for her to gaze upon them fully without turning away. They made her uncomfortable by the intensity of their loveliness. In the spring her mother would search out the plants in the woods, bringing a few home in a moss-lined basket. The rock garden was cool, protected by the pines, near thirty feet tall, that surrounded the house. When the wind ran through the tops of them, the soughing mingling with the sound of the high waves from below the dune, the girl would sit and listen, liking the sounds. But now the pines were standing still and sullen; they waited for the sun to be gone, falling in a pool of blood into the lake.

"Can I borrow your knife?" she asked.

The boy unsnapped it from his belt. "It's very sharp."

She unfolded the narrowest blade and sat forward on her hips. She slit the underskin of the black-and-white pig first, careful not to sever the organs. She slid out two tiny bodies, one a mottled tricolor, the other white with pink eyes. On the air, like the cooing of doves in a cote, came her sisters' prattle. *Coo-roo. Coo-too-roo.* The girl turned over the brown-and-white one next and there were four babies. She had suspected quads and sensed a pride at the fertility displayed. Two were black like the male and one a spotted brown. But the last was wee and of a color she had never seen before, a sort of yellow with rusty speckles. She turned the old ones' bodies so the cuts didn't show. "That last baby is a very highly unusual color." She tried to keep her lips from twisting when she said it. She turned her head from the boy and drove his knife repeatedly into the dirt to clean the blade. She wiped it on the grass and gave it to him. "I would have had ten cavies!" She was compounding her grief. Purposely she'd increased the corpses, gloating over the lost, the many lovely dead, mourning ten, not four.

The boy looked down at her bent shoulders, at her spoiled crumpled dress. He cleared his throat. "We ought to bury them. Do you want to hold a funeral?"

"Yes," she said and caught her breath. Suddenly she was crying, putting her head on her knees. "Darn those dogs, anyway!"

"Should I get a spade from the garage?"

She lifted her head considering, and the tears ceased. "I have a place where I bury things."

He accepted it. "Okay. I'll get a spade and you find something to put them in."

"You won't let the dogs get at them again?"

"No. Hurry. It's near suppertime."

She ran, suddenly eager. She hunted out four shoe boxes and ribbon and cotton. She joined him where he stood guard at the step. She arranged the dead, placing the babies with their proper mothers. And she strung ribbons about them, and put

---

The Grandmother

the lids on. They walked swiftly through the woods, the boxes under their arms. She shoved the spiny branches aside and showed him the woodspot in the center.

"Who'd ever have thought there was a clearing in here. You'd never suspect it from the outside."

She knew he was trying to comfort her and that made the hard bump rise again in her throat. He was spading an oblong hole. They uncovered the coffins and set them in a row. She leaned over to touch the tiniest yellow baby with her finger. "This one is pretty! What a funny color." The cavy had such beauty that a pang cleaved through her. The lump in her throat got larger and she made a face, almost in tears.

The boy stood very tall and spoke like a minister. "These innocents were taken from this lady by God. They have been massacred by a wild clan of huns. Ours is not to reason why!"

She started crying again and the lump refused to melt. She tried swallowing it because her throat hurt. The scent of evergreens was biting and redolent, and the damp earth pungent. No sun ever shone in this place and the ground was cushioned with crumbled brown needles. The boy was replacing the covers and putting the boxes in the grave. His movements were swift and graceful, and she felt how she would always be his slave. Even if he hated her sometime. Her loyalty would be undying. He sprinkled dirt upon the boxes. "Earth to earth," he declared. "That's what they always say."

When he was finished they sat on the ground for a while. She broke the stillness. "Ten cavies. I have to put a marker up for them."

"Did you mind me saying that about huns? I wasn't insulting your sisters' dogs."

"No. Darn them!"

"I wouldn't mind chiseling that epitaph in stone," he offered.

She felt the companionship, in the fragrant shade, secluded from the sun that moved actively beyond this green womb of trees. She felt the fullness of her emotion, and said dreamily, "That would be neat. Thanks."

"What would you want on it?"

"Dearly loved, I guess." And again there loomed the blackness of her failure. "It was my fault! I left the door off."

"You didn't mean to."

"Yes, but I did! I shouldn't blame the dogs. It was me. I killed them."

"I called you away. So it's my fault."

"No." She felt the depth of her loss, but there was a new sweetness in it since he claimed a piece of the blame.

The boy got up. "Let's go now. It's late."

"Okay."

On their way out, he held the heavy limbs aside for her, the first tribute of that kind he'd ever paid her. She was chief mourner here. As they approached *The Manse*, two of her sisters plunged from the doorway, their dogs scampering beside them. The eldest was shading her hand, standing within the screen. "Where were you? Where did you go? Gran died. We wanted to tell you the news!" Their father had called more than an hour ago. "You should know about it. Isn't it terrible?" They watched their littlest sister to see the effect their words would have.

She felt her distinction before the boy, in one more loss. People might laugh if you grieved over losing your pets, but not when it was your grandmother. That was sure. But his mien was sober. "I suppose you don't feel like finishing the tennis set now?" he asked.

"But, gee, I do. Thanks for asking. Let me get my soft shoes. Can you wait a sec?" Full speed, she was dashing up the stairs to her room, to leave the stained dress in a heap and to change into fresh shorts and shirt. His twin, in white.

She slammed the door behind her and was running down. They were racing to the court. Her racket was on the bench.

The Grandmother

Someone had picked it up and laid it there. The boy and she were vigorous and when a breeze sprang up they laughed, filling their lungs and shouting louder than they ever had before. Their calls rang through the treetops. Their bodies were intense, and it was as if a joy were binding them and release could come only through violent movements and wild cries. She served for the first time in the hard overhand stroke he used. Whack! The ball was inside and he yelled, returning it, "Nice serve!" They were fearless and strong, and they didn't know why.

Mary Had a Redbird

I could tell I was quite a bit taller than the boy. I sat down beside him after we got on at the Cleveland depot. I got my growth early; I've been captain of the basketball team for two years. Aunt Betty Lou and Albert and Evans had taken seats together in back, and this was the only one left. It was a good one, the second behind the green, thick glass that looks into the treetops from the top story of the stratodome bus. You could see the shapes of the leaves and the high, secret branches. It gave you a new way of looking at things.

The first thing he did when I told him my name was to laugh, "Who ever heard of such a funny one."

"For Angeline," I said, looking past him at the countryside, which is very ordinary outside Cleveland.

The boy's gurgle burst again from him, "Angie!"

He'd been silent as we rumbled through the city traffic. Now we were on the turnpike in the green hilled country, with depressions and dells standing out black and shadowy. It was sticky hot outside, but in here air conditioning made it almost cold.

"What's yours?" I asked carefully.

"Paul. I been on a different express every day for five days now." Everything he said sort of tickled him. Blond, small-boned, he seemed underfed. His skin was pretty and pale. He moved about in the prickly upholstered seat as if he were chained.

I turned around to see what my aunt was doing. She gazed out the way a foreigner might, to whom all the scenery was new. She wouldn't lean back the whole way to Washington, D.C. She looked as though she was waiting for someone to take her by surprise. Her skin was polished and shiny; her gray hair was pulled back in a strict knot, her nose was like a hawk's beak and she almost never smiled. Because of corns, she'd slipped into cloth shoes the minute the bus started. Her suit wouldn't have a wrinkle when we finally arrived the way mine would have from sitting too long.

Paul looked ready to laugh again. He asked me, "How old would you be, anyhow?"

"Thirteen in May."

"Then we're the same age. Where from?"

"I was brought up in Chicago. Say, you like to talk."

"Shee-cah-go!" Paul mimicked me. "Angie comes from Shee-cah-go."

"So what?"

He moved his thin knees, separating them. "Look here."

"Let's see." I leaned over. On the floor was a cage, toy birds on the perches.

"Pop gave it to me before I left. Bought it in Europe, I think. Watch out." Dragging it up, trying to be gentle, he jerked it past his legs and balanced it on his lap. It was thin-wired and dome-shaped, golden.

"Well, I'll be." It was a splendid thing. The bird feathers and skins had been glued over frames so they looked alive. The big one was red and the other yellow, and there were pretty feathered crests and long tails.

"I've got a key somewhere." Paul was fishing in his pockets. After much searching, he brought out an object which he offered. "Here."

I took it in my palm to look. It was odd-shaped, gilded; I wondered how it made the birds sing. "Can I wind it?"

"Look at your hand." Curious, he was touching the pinkish inside of mine where the key lay, smoothing it.

My fast anger came up in me. "Look at yours!" I flicked the key back at him. It hit the cage tinkling and was lost on the seat between us.

He hunted for it, getting up. "Here, Angie." He pushed it into my hand. I let him. His face crinkled in a smile, his sky-blue eyes friendly. Way down in them was a flicker like red, and I wondered if Paul was lonely. Suddenly I was feeling sorry for him instead of having pity for myself. I used to make up stories lying in bed at night about turning white in the morning. My doll was white and Santa Claus was, and so were angels. When Aunt Betty Lou caught me at the mirror she said did I think white persons were all satisfied? Didn't I have two eyes and two ears and one nose? I knew what she was telling me: I was lucky to be me. And this minute she was watching over me back there like a big old broody bird. And my brothers were waiting for me to play with them.

"Do you always travel alone?" I asked Paul.

"Oh, sure. Twice a year. L.A. to D.C. and back. My mother sells real estate; she has this apartment in Washington. Summers I go visit my father. The way I said, this year he gave me this cage when I asked for it. Feature that."

"Who do you like the best of your parents?"

"Pop. That's easy. I get in Mother's way. She's getting married again." He made a face, laughing as if it were funny. "Who do you like?"

"I just have an aunt. I live with her."

He twisted his body up sideways to look back. "She her?" He said it respectfully, earnest.

"Um." I was thinking Aunt Betty Lou'd like him fine if they ever got to know each other.

He tapped the cage. "Clear from Cali-for-ny-ay with this thing. Silly to travel with it but I don't care. Hope it doesn't get broken before I get there."

"That would be awful."

"Ah-ful!" He slid down in his seat, mocking me again. He gazed up through the pink glass of the skylight.

"Do you like riding buses?"

"Wish you'd have seen the one from Denver to Omaha, Angie. I thought I was doomed to spend the rest of my life in Nebraska. It was hot! Trouble was, the passengers kept opening windows. When we stopped to eat, the driver and me went around and closed them so the air conditioner could operate. But the second they got back, up they went again." He bounced the cage on his lap, full of energy.

I had the key tight in my hand. I pulled at my skirt so it covered my smooth honey knees. One of my faults is I'm vain. I liked my red suit which was new for the trip. I'd bobbed my hair about a month ago. I crossed my ankles, conscious of my new patent leather slippers. "Okay to wind it, Paul?"

"Poll? Say Paul, not Poll!"

I tried. "Poll!"

"I give up. You're hopeless. Aren't we in Pittsburgh yet?" He looked out, pushing the cage toward me. "Sure, wind it."

I stuck the key in its place. I like locks and keys, the way one key will fit one lock and no other. As I turned the metal around, it clicked loudly. "Do they really sing?"

"You'll see." We were coming into a small town. The driver pressed the horn—*Rawk, hawk!* Far away, down in the street, we could look into the upper stories of houses where bare bulbs hung, and worn, green shades tilted sidewise. An old man in a T shirt leaned on his elbows to watch us go by. *Rawk!* Outside on the sidewalk a teen-age boy was passing. Paul signaled silently and wildly to him, letting the cage go and gluing his forehead to the pane. "Did you see that, Angie?" Paul wheeled. "He waved back!"

"Make them sing."

"Press the lever here."

The insides of their beaks were painted bright red. Their toes were pasted onto the dusty perches; their features looked ruffled and worn as if the toy had been made years ago. *"Bee-dee-dee-dee-deeeee!"* Bills opening, closing, bodies bobbing, first one and then the other.

"Well, I'll be."

Paul nudged me with his sharp elbow. "Crazy?"

"Um!"

They ran down, jerking slower and slower and then quitting altogether. We sat without saying anything for a while; it was as if Paul's vigor stilled with theirs. Around us many had been lulled to sleep by the bus motion, heads lolling on arms, pillows, shoulders. Children crayoned and chewed gum; a baby whined. We were entering the outskirts of Pittsburgh.

"Want to wind them up again, Angie?"

I turned the key and we sat back. When the bus braked in the Greyhound yard, the driver's voice through the loudspeaker overrode the dying peeps. "Passengers bound for New York will change here." People left their seats, beginning to chatter as their bodies awoke. I felt fingers on my right, plucking my sleeve. My brother. The driver droned on. "Passengers bound for Hagerstown, Frederick, Washington, remain in your seats. Do not disembark. This is not a comfort stop."

Albert bent his head to me. "Come on, Angie! We've got a seat for you. We're saving it." Albert's ten, big for his age. His manners are middling and he's very set.

"No. This is fine."

He pulled sharply at my sleeve again. "Aunt Betty Lou said for you to. We're holding your seat." Then he pinched my flesh anxiously. "Angie, please!" I held my mouth firm. After a minute he gave up. "Huh!" He knows how willful I am at times.

"Who's that?" Paul asked. "Your brother?"

"Albert. I'll get him tonight."

"What's he like to do best?"

"Baseball. He's in the Little League. Pitcher. You belong to a league?"

"Nope."

"Albert's a left-handed pitcher." I looked in Paul's eyes, seeing the red again down deep.

"Getting hot. Why don't they close the door!" Paul moved around on his seat, jolting the cage up and down. The feathers on the birds' heads wavered and the metal cage rattled. "Let's go, driver!"

"Yeah," I laughed. "Come on, driver."

Paul imitated me. "Come ahn, driver."

The motor roared up under us. Right away I got that feeling that comes over me when I'm on the way again into a new place or thought. You never can tell where the glory lies; you might stumble on it anywhere. That's what Aunt Betty Lou says. It can be there in the black of night when the curtain moves and the moon enters the window like a squashed cherry. It can strike on the middle of a white street when the daytime moon's a piece of paper and you feel your place in the tide of living and dead. Or even riding along in this stratodome express. I hummed, tapping my toe. "*Mary wore a red dress, red dress, red dress—Mary wore a red dress all day long!*"

"Angie, what's that? It's crazy."

"Oh, some old song."

"Sing it."

"*Mary had a redbird, redbird, redbird—Mary had a redbird all day long!*"

Paul laughed. "Ahl day lahng!"

The Pennsylvania countryside was changing as it does when you reach the mountains. We rode higher and higher. Mist came off the Appalachians in long streamers that trailed like balloon strings. You could see fifty miles away and way, way down. We groaned up the grades and dashed pell-mell down.

There were fields of Queen Anne's lace and hillside farms with crooked buildings. Paul put the bird cage down and began to point out places he knew, telling what was coming next. He'd made the trip so many times he even knew billboards and signs. He put his finger on the green glass. "That's Jim's Vista. You can see four states on a clear day."

"Name them. I'll bet you can't."

"Maryland, Pennsylvania and Virginia . . ."

"I'll be."

"And West Virginia."

The driver cleared his throat over the speaker. "There will be a fifteen-minute comfort stop in McConnellsburg."

"I'll stay here, Paul. And save the seats."

"No one'll take them. Come on. I'm thirsty."

"I'll just stay. I'm not."

"Suit yourself." He climbed over my legs into the aisle and was gone in the line of passengers shuffling down the inside stairs and out into the sun-ripped day.

There were my brothers in the aisle. "Hey, Angie!" Evans lisped. He's six, his smile white in his light face.

Albert crowded him, mad. "Why didn't you sit with us! Why do you have to talk with him?"

"Hey, Angie," Evans said again and we grinned at each other.

Albert whispered, "Aunt Betty Lou said tell you she's not speaking with you."

But I stuck Evans in the ribs. He's the baby of us three and can't bear to be tickled. He gave a shriek of pleasure. Albert took his hand. "Hush. Hush." They were shoved and hustled away. Soon only a few passengers remained in the seats. I didn't look around; I could feel my aunt's still eyes in the back seat.

When Paul got back he was balancing an orange drink in a paper cup. "Thought you might be thirsty by now, Miss Ahngie!" He was chuckling, handing it to me. "I had two giant hot dogs with pickles and relish and the works." He clambered into his seat, squeezing his body to avoid the cage on the floor and the cup in my hands. "And a Grapelade. I keep myself stuffed but I stay skinny all the time."

"Thanks." I fumbled for the coin purse in my jacket pocket. "I think I have a dime."

"Crazy, it's a treat."

I let my purse go and sipped the ice-cold sweet liquid. I was feeling tight and wound-up inside like a ball of string.

The sun glazed brilliant. As we roared on, the mountains were replaced in time by Washington's soot-grimed streets bordered by white buildings and old green trees, gas pumps and signs. We moved uncertainly, jerking and changing gears at traffic lights and corners. The driver's voice growled, "All passengers will disembark." We swung into the terminal lot where white stripes marked each lane. Paul reached for the cage. "This is it, D.C., one more time!"

"Your mother meeting you?"

"She's busy. I don't care. I'm crazy. I don't even phone. Just take the streetcar up to the apartment and the janitor's wife lets me in." He grinned as he got into the aisle in front of me. "Now, I'll see you around town, Ahngeline."

"Yeah!"

He was going down the inside steps ahead, the cage clutched under his arm. As he went through the folded doors, he turned and lifted a wispy, cheerful hand in salute. "So long."

"Yeah."

I went over by the station wall to wait for Aunt Betty Lou. She came, waving the baggage checks. She'd put on her hat with the flowers of purple and white that she kept clean in a paper sack on the rack over her seat. She walked stiffly, for she'd changed back into her best shoes, black and laced high on the instep. Leaning over, she pulled straight the wrinkles in her lisle stockings. The porter was opening the side of the bus where the luggage was stored.

My aunt's voice was firm. "I said you ought not to talk with white boys."

"Why? Why?"

Aunt Betty Lou was already taking her suitcase and walking into the station where my brother would be slipping pennies in the slot of the gum machine.

"But why?"

A stratodome bus was pulling out of the line. The driver was revving the engine and its crazy thunder made the sidewalk under me tremble like glory. The tight ball was already beginning to unravel as I went through the terminal building door.

Witch Chicken

He had lost his way in the valley, for three years' growth had put a new face over the June landscape. One of the clay-eaters gave him directions. There were a group of them with paper bags and spoons, getting a supply of the white hearth clay to take back to their cabins. The skin of one was pulled tight across the bones of her face. She held one hand half over her mouth to hide the bulge in her cheek where the clay was wadded.

"Where's the Tolliver cabin?" he asked her, and wiped the sweat from his face with a large blue kerchief. "Tremble Tolliver, the chair maker."

He waited for an answer, hitching the black galluses that held up his green pants. His yellow shirt was limp from the movements his body made as he walked, as though the starch were whipped from it. The jackass he had passed a stitch back on the road brayed again. The woman at length spoke in a long whine:

"Hold to the pike till you come on the burial ground, Mester, set about with simmon trees. Then bear right and keep climbing up the Shoestring. It's on the other side."

"Much obliged," he said and whispered, "I remember now." He stuffed the kerchief in his back pocket. It was then that a sound came up like shouting and wild clanging somewhere in the valley. He wondered what was its cause.

The hot perfume of the morning wind swept along the earth.

The ass could still be heard braying but the sound came fainter now, replaced by the bell-song of the wood thrush close at hand, and the two-toned clangor of the blue jay in the undergrowth and timber that crowded the road skirting the foot of the mountain.

The dust of the pike was unsettled by his heavy-soled shoes. It rose to hover in the air behind the tall striding figure. The breeze had just died. In a swinging movement, the man changed hands holding his black satchel. It contained a fresh yellow shirt, a razor, his Bible, and order books. He had risen early and walked all the way from the town of Four Valleys that morning, near ten miles. He halted in the road and pulled out his watch. His thumbnail flipped the lid on which was engraved a stag with lowered antlers. The man was proud of his moon calendar watch and used it as a conversation piece while making his sales or taking orders. It was Swiss-made and had cost six dollars, thirty cents. He nodded to it.

But then his thin elongated face drew into a frown and his eyes darkened. He seemed to glimpse a moment into the future where the weary years dragged. He shook his head and muttered:

"The lot is cast into the lap but the whole disposing thereof is of the Lord."

He began to sing to cheer himself, and his legs, which a girl had once said were like those of the long-legged harvestman spider, ate up the miles:

> "*All the trees they are so high*
> *The leaves they are so green*
> *The day is past and gone, sweetheart*
> *That you and I have seen!*
>
> "*I saw the new moon late yestreen*
> *With the old moon in her arm*
> *And if we go to sea, master*
> *I fear we'll come to harm!*"

Witch Chicken

At the burial ground he turned as the clay-eater had directed. He recalled that when he'd last seen it three years ago it had been a pretty spot, well tended. Now it was a patch of rubble. Beyond was the grove of persimmon trees, stark shafts covered with black bark, and with twisted branches. The community no longer used this ground since a new graveyard had been laid out by the big Baptist church in Four Valleys. Folks had uprooted most of the old bones and moved them to the new ground. It was the remains of the exceeding poor or of those who had no one to care, or of the ones who had been forgot in the wake of time that mouldered here amid gaping excavations.

Of a sudden a blind owl flapped across the lot before him, on brown soft wings. The man turned away and began to climb the steep rutted mule path up Shoestring Mountain.

Sedgegrass and mullein grew in the unworn way, and blooming wild spikenards and thistles. A woodchuck waddled down the path. It scuttled back on sight of the tall man, its black heels flashing in the sun as it ran for its hole in a rotted stump. There it turned to chatter in defiance, its bobbing nose visible.

At the mountain crest there was a rock precipice. The honeysuckle odor that drifted up from the valley was overpowering. He stood catching his breath. I'm going on forty, he thought, not as young as I once was. Used to make the hill and never blow. He looked and it seemed the land spread out like a patchwork quilt, brown and yellow and green where cornfields and tobacco patches and garden plots were made into rectangles. They were, he fancied, such as a mountain girl might have pieced to make a quilt and then give it a name as was their custom, like *Rob Peter to Pay Paul* or *Dove at the Window*. And it was hemstitched by rail fences and tree rows and hedges, and now and then a small cabin to vary the design.

He mused while smelling the flowers and admiring the far country. Then he heard a laugh that he remembered. It came again, and he followed where it led; he went, he thought, in the

---

Children and Lovers

way that a piece of iron will slip right to the horseshoe magnet, the kind he'd played with when he was a little tad.

He parted the haw bushes to look within. There a young girl and her lover played. She was lying in the grass, clad in a one-piece linsey-woolsey dress like the mountain girls wear. She was barefooted. Her black hair hung like a river about her shoulders. It was long and shining and not held by any band. Above her kneeled a strapping fellow of nineteen or thereabouts, black-headed, and with large angular hands. His hair was grown shaggy on his neck. His mouth was broad and laughed, and his eyes were bent on her. He held her shoulders with his great fingers. What he thought of her bloomed from his eyes.

"Will!" She laughed again. "You win. You are strong!" He released her, and she sat up in the grass.

"Dulcie Tolliver," the tall man breathed to himself. He turned again to the path for he saw the girl's sweetheart moving to kiss her, and he wouldn't spy on that. He traveled down from the head of the mountain, his steps now lagging and his head bent in thought. He had business at the Tolliver cabin. He had come to give Tremble Tolliver his chair order for the next year and to see what his wife, Sal, had to offer in the way of weaving. He felt old. It was the sight of the girl in the haw thicket that made him feel that way. He was a bachelor. The only one he ever wanted wouldn't have him, though he'd wooed her in the finest way he knew. He'd thought to sweep her from her feet as he had been swept at first sight of her.

The other Tolliver daughter was a dummy, he recalled. They wouldn't let her work the looms for she couldn't remember a change and either stopped her weaving or continued in the same way and spoiled the pattern. The dummy was but good to mind the sheep, and sometimes she helped Sal gather the honeysuckle vines she wove into baskets to sell.

Ahead was the cabin. He remembered it at once, set snug in the clearing. It was a but-and-ben, made of two cabins, each a single room with a loft above, and joined by a roof of narrow boards, split with a froe. The Tollivers called the passageway between the dog trot. The chimneys were built of logs and clay, and neither room nor loft had a window to grace it. Alongside the fireplace though, there was an opening the height of two logs. You could sit there of a night before the hearth and see the stars and the fire glittering at the same time, in a friendly way. The front and back doors were swung on strips of animal skin, and the dwelling was so placed that in the early frost of a morning the sun ball came into the room through one doorway. And of an evening, the rays crept through the other one and along the floor until the cabin was flooded yellow clear out to the yard on the other side. Then you watched the sphere like a ripe persimmon sink in the westerly sky.

"The house of the righteous is much treasure," he murmured.

The loom was clacking as he came across the clearing. It was Sal Tolliver in the cabin, he thought, her delicate hands working the loom, weaving the coverlets for him to sell. Tremble sat outside the dog trot that was piled high now with his fine-made chairs. He looked up when he saw the long-legged man coming across the yard, swinging his satchel and his yellow hair standing up like a thatch. Tremble was a wizened bit of a man. He looked back down at the strips of corn husk he was weaving into the bottom of a chair. It was said that Tremble Tolliver's chairs couldn't be worn out. There was no piece of metal in them. It was like they had grown in one piece.

Tremble nodded. "I've been looking for you since the new moon came on, Lem Adam. Have a chair." He took up a new strip from the great heap of husks just under the roof. He smoothed it straight with his hand.

"I'll do that, Mester Tolliver." The man threw down his satchel.

Tremble shouted, "Jessemine! Bring a piggin of milk. We've got company!"

Lem Adam knew the dummy would take awhile. He lifted one of the chairs down from the pile and rested himself. Then he saw Dulcie Tolliver walking across the clearing from the woods beyond. "Now there's your daughter coming," Lem said.

Tremble grunted, and the man thought, Dulcie ever did have an air. Her face was smooth like a balmy sky. It was even-featured and the color in her cheeks, not brash like some, was just tinged, like the snow apple. That's the one which comes late and has a tempered color to it like it begged your leave politely. Once he'd said that to her and she'd laughed at him.

The girl approached. She looked at Lem from under her long lashes. He could never tell the color of her eyes for she kept them downcast. This had always been a tantalizement to him. He would look for ways to make her lift them. They sparkled now through the black lashes, so he knew she had seen him spying in the haw thicket awhile ago.

"Morning, Dulcie," he said, "I came to get your Pa's order."

"It's been a spell since I laid eyes on you, Mester Adam!"

"Your Ma's looking for you," said Tremble.

And the girl passed into the cabin. She could be heard talking to Sal. The loom never ceased in its clicking as the shuttle was passed through the shed of the warp, weaving the web. The yellow-haired man sat with the flush high on him, for so the girl had always affected him.

"It's been long since you've been here," said Tremble.

"They gave me this beat again. I asked for it. I took a notion to see the mountains again."

"Where've you been working?"

"Been covering small towns, mostly in west Kentucky."

"What's it like in the lowlands?"

"Lots of people."

"I've never been past Four Valleys, hauling the chairs and such down once a year."

"I came back to see the mountains."

"The dealer that came last year said you'd be back."

Witch Chicken

"Here I am." Lem listened to the girl within.

Jessemine came bearing the bowl of milk.

"I'm obliged," Lem said, taking it.

The young girl stood twisting her bare feet one on the other. Her dark hair that her mother had combed hung roughly at the sides.

"You can go in the cabin," Tremble told her, for she seemed to be waiting.

"I will, Pa." She went within to sit on the bench and hold her poppet-doll in her hands, twisting it silently.

"Got news," Tremble said. "Dulcie's getting wedded."

The man started, moving his lanky body restively. "No."

"Yes. And the boy's in a swivet to get it over."

"When?" I should have stayed in the west, he thought. Why'd I come looking for her again?

"She's taking that young Will Hamm. He built them a cabin at the foot of the Shoestring. The land's been cleared. The boy put in a cornfield and now's he's messing with a patch of tobacco. He's burned it off proper and it's all in bloom now, a sight to see!" Tremble dwelled on the young folks' plans. "I gave them a young ram and two ewes to start their own flock so Dulcie can spin like Sal. There's a little field of flax planted for her too."

The man stirred. He wasn't listening. Tremble sighed, "Reckon Sal and me'll miss Dulcie's singing all the day."

The girl's voice, following his words, rose quavering sweet through the doorway. The two men sat in the noonday sun with the clinging scent of the honeysuckle sweeping over the top of the mountain. It seemed to Lem Adam that the song sat like a crown on them:

> *"Down in yon valley there grows a green arrow;*
> *I wish that arrow was shot through my breast;*
> *It would end my grief, it would end my sorrow;*
> *It would set my troubled mind at rest!"*

That evening, at the table, the light of the setting sun flowed over the puncheon floor that had been smoothed by shoes and bare feet over the years. Sal moved about heavily. She told Jessemine to take her chair and she gave her a dish. There was warm cornbread and fresh-churned butter and a pitcher of sweet milk set out. While they ate, the man saw that the faces of the parents turned, like sunflowers that follow the dazzling ball of light across its bow in a day, to Dulcie. She looked through her lashes at him:

"We're weaving my marriage counterpane."

"I just now heard of your wedding," he said.

"It'll be ready tomorrow," she told him.

"Its pattern is named *The Rose of the Mountain*," Sal broke in. "That Will Hamm, he'll stand over there and watch her loom working. Rose of the mountain, he'll say, that counterpane's trying to rival your face today!" Sal was pleased.

"O, Ma!" Dulcie cried, and she laughed.

After the dishes were cleared, the girl went to the finger-shuttle loom. Her hands roved swiftly over her wedding coverlet. Lem Adam stood by and watched her as the shuttle passed swiftly to and fro. She paused in the rhythm to lay in a design and then picked up the shuttle again to make it travel.

"See there at those rosebuds!" She tromped the treadle. "Coming in like the first sun of morning will bring them into blow."

"It's fair," he murmured.

"Weaving, Mester Adam, is the prettiest work ever!"

He turned abruptly to the glowing fire that Tremble had made to cut the night damp of the mountain and the coolness that was descending. The fire burned to a glowing ash. The stars fluttered in the peephole beside the fireplace. Tremble and he sat before it, their pipes lit and the blue smoke sifting over them. Sal was on a bench at the side with Jessemine. She watched Dulcie while she rested.

At length Sal spoke, "Let it go for tonight. You've got time a-plenty tomorrow."

"All right, Ma." The click of the loom ceased, and the girl arose. She went to look out the peephole. "I heard the German today."

"Who's he?" Lem asked.

"He's the honey-man."

"He's got droves of bees," Tremble told him, "and when the sound comes up from the valley of a far-off commotion, you know his bees are swarming."

"They beat pans," said Sal, "and blow horns and shout."

"I heard them when I came over the pike. I'd just passed the clay-eaters. I wondered what it was."

"A swarm of bees in June," the dummy piped up, "is worth a silver spoon." She turned back to her doll.

"That noise is to drown the call of the queen."

"I see," said Lem.

"So the bees will stay with the hive."

"Jessemine." Sal put her hand to her hair that was drawn into a bun. "Let's go to bed."

"Yes, Ma."

"Good night," Lem said.

The two went out into the dog trot to the other cabin where they slept. Tremble got up and began to bank the coals for the next morning's fire.

"Do I sleep down here, Mester Tolliver?" asked the tall man.

"Where's our manners, Dulcie! Show Lem Adam his bed."

The girl turned from the opening in the logs. "You'll sleep in this loft tonight, Mester Adam."

She lit a candle. He took his satchel and followed her up the ladder. The shadows fluttered over them like birds. There were no carpets or rugs for the floors and no decorations in the Tolliver cabin. But Sal had a fame for fine counterpanes. City folk laid them over their beds, harking back to old unhurried days. Sal and Dulcie cut the wool from the sheep. They washed and carded it, and then dyed it with Tremble's help and spun it. Linen thread they spun too from flax which throve in this region. Combined with wool the flax made up into linsey-woolsey.

Lem went up the ladder now after Dulcie. Three years ago he'd slept in the other cabin. He'd never been in this loft. He stopped at the head, for by the light of the candle, he saw that a kingly room was arranged for a traveler who might come to spend a night. The floor of the sleeping loft was spread with finely contrived patchwork quilts and coverlets, some of them worn nearly to shreds. He plucked off his shoes and strode boldly to the middle of the shadowy room. Wherever he stood were the tiny threads that were stitched and spun and woven by the woman and her daughter. He studied the patterns and the colors and how they were combined in their separate ways. On the pallet of corn husks more were piled. A night breeze blew through the openings under the roof-eaves.

The girl cried to him from where she stood holding the candle:

"You're gangly like a harvestman spider. I always said it! Look there at your shadow."

"I know it's an ugly one!" He glanced behind where like a tottering giant, it crept upon the crossbeams of the slanted roof.

"I'll say good night."

"Wait, Dulcie! Call the patterns over to me."

"All right. This one's *Bachelor's Delight,* and here is *Doors and Windows,* and *Eight Ways of Contrariness.*" She stepped about in the flicker of light, pointing with her bare foot. "And *Job's Trouble* and *Owsley's Forks.*"

"I know this one," he whispered. "It's *Young Man's Sorrow.* Don't go!" he cried as she slipped to the head of the ladder.

"That one's *Roses and Pinies in the Wilderness,*" she said gently.

"How do you make the colors, Dulcie?"

"The pink-yellow color here." She knelt to touch with her finger a stripe in the design. "Comes from that ugly sedge grass. You'd not think it could make such a surprising color." She held the candlestick in her other hand and by the uncertain light it seemed to the man as if she were a figure from a dream.

"I'm thinking of the summer three years past, Dulcie."

"Pokeberry makes this lavendery."

"I came back to see if you'd change your mind. When will you be wedded?"

"Day after tomorrow. And if you take great care, it makes a pretty pink."

"So soon! There's not another like you, Dulcie!"

"Black is from the butternut hulls."

"I saw you in the hawthorn thicket."

"I know it. Good night."

And she was gone down the crude ladder. He stretched his length out on the pallet in the regal chamber. The soft steps of the girl whispered as she went across the clearing away from the cabin. The sound mingled into the honeysuckle's palpable odor. He took his Bible from the satchel and read by the flicker of light.

In the morning Lem went out to the pump to wash. He put his blond head into the stream of water. As he lifted it dripping, he saw Dulcie come from the mountain path, carrying a wood trencher of foaming milk in her hand. She was laughing, and she held her sister's hand and made her smile too. He shook the water from his hair and called:

"Morning!"

The dummy broke loose from Dulcie and ran to him. "We saw a witch chicken!" Her vacant eyes glinted with excitement.

"We did." Dulcie came up. "When I was milking the cow. I'm glad our hens have got a shed to hide in."

"That owl's bound to catch chickens," Lem laughed at them, "for his livelihood. Why call him a witch?"

"And Dulcie talked to him!" said Jessemine.

"What did you tell him, Dulcie?"

"I said, *Old Tom Walker under your hat! Father, Son, and Holy Ghost!*"

"Do you believe in those old spells, Dulcie?"

The girl ceased her laughter. She looked out to the woods where the cow roamed. A cloud moved across the sun so that a shadow touched her face.

"It can't hurt."

She turned away, and the dummy followed her into the cabin. The man bent over the pump again and finished his washing. Later while the looms were busy, the two men talked business. They came to an agreement on prices for Tremble's chairs and Sal's weaving and the egg baskets she made from honeysuckle vines, boiling off the bark and trimming the knots. Lem put the orders away in his satchel.

"I must get back down the mountain." He arose.

"Stay for the noonday meal."

"Well, much obliged," Lem said quickly, for his life was a lonely one. He folded himself onto the bench by the door again.

Tremble began telling long-drawn tales. Lem listened. The brassy sun shone, and Tremble worked carefully with his hands, nodding, and now and then pausing to wave. He told of the early settlers, of the great licks where the animals congregated and one could shoot any kind of game he pleased, wildcats and wolves, buffalo and giant elk, bear and deer, and almost any of the small varmints that gathered to satisfy their craving for salt.

"And there's the preacher now." Tremble's old face crumpled in a grin. "He'd nine children when his wife took and died. Preacher married a widow lady with thirteen. Now how'd you like to see that crowd setting up to table?"

"Twenty-two brats," Lem sighed, stretching his legs.

The Holy Rollers had come to Four Valleys, Tremble said, and got in with the law for breaking the peace. They handled snakes and white-hot lamp chimneys. They got the shakes and jabber-jabbered in the unknown tongue. Then he talked about Dulcie, and his face softened.

"Will you be buying counterpanes off her when she's Will Hamm's wife? She favors the trade of weaving."

"I will, Mester Tolliver."

"If you come back in a year, maybe there'll be a little lap-baby around."

"Children's children are the crown of old men." Lem Adam was given to heavy quotations that he read in his Bible on the long evenings. "And the glory of children are their fathers."

"A glory," Tremble mumbled and gazed into the pale sunrays on the weeds.

It seemed to Lem that while the old man dreamed, a haze drifted across the sun and there was an evil betokened by it. I've no second sight for the future, he thought, and it may just be the fear that clutches us poor mortals through this journey of darkness, for those we love. So a mother fears when her small ones are playing near the wood. "Perhaps just now," she will say, "one has fallen and hurt himself. Perhaps an unknown beast has come upon them." And she will run to see them stringing chains from the feverfews and daisies and crowning one another there in the safe meadow. So Lem Adam felt when the mist passed over the sky just then. Is there a danger to one I love well? He spoke softly:

"Tell me, what's a witch chicken, Mester Tolliver?"

"What say? Why that's a mean hoot owl. They've got a way of coming soft into a tree where the hens roost. They'll nudge the fowl till she slips off the branch, and when she falls, the witch chicken'll grab her in midair. His talons are the size of a man's hand. He'll flap off with her."

Jessemine came to bid them eat. The two men went slowly in. When they had finished, Dulcie asked:

"Shall I walk to the mountaintop with you, Mester Adam? I know a doves' nest in the face of the cliff."

"I'd think it a favor."

So he took up his black satchel and bid the Tollivers good-
bye for the year. He went up the path with her. Ever after, he
remembered how the breezes were bound to outdo themselves
and vied for first place in the girl's black hair that streamed
glossy. She walked with her head down, hiding the color of her
eyes from him. She skipped on the path so that he felt his age
on him again, like an old man who held a child from her
accustomed gait.

"Dulcie!" The yellow-haired man stopped on the path. "I
didn't know you'd been promised."

Her young ways dropped from her and she said gravely, "I
know it."

"So I came unprepared." He drew from his pocket the moon
calendar watch. "But I make you a wedding gift of this. Thus
you open it." He showed her with his fingernail.

"O, I couldn't take that."

He held it out. "It keeps tab of the day of week, the day of
month, and the month of year." His narrow face was eager.

"No! It's too fine."

"And the changes of moon. It was made across the water."

"Can't you stay over a day for the wedding?" She accepted
the present.

"No, I have to go. I have business."

They walked again, and she beside him, tuning her gait to
his. They came to the head of Shoestring Mountain. The
patchwork quilt of farmland was spread before. He threw his
gangly arms out boldly:

"Name that quilt, Dulcie!"

"I name it *Beauty of Kaintuck*," she said on the instant. "For
I favor that patchwork valley. My favorite pattern's *The Rose
of the Mountain*, though." She looked through her lashes, and
he knew Dulcie said it because of Will Hamm's telling her the
counterpane wanted to be like her, she was so fair.

"There's the dove's nest. See?" She pointed to a ledge under the side of the mountain below where they stood. "The nestlings are almost ready to leave. Their breasts are a pinkish-gray."

"Let them be!"

"I want you to see, Lem."

He knew she called him by his given name on purpose because of the pain of his final parting with her.

"I don't care to."

But she laughed and scrambled down to the nest. She took up a dove and spoke to it; it lay quiet in her hand. From afar the parent bird's doleful coo was heard. A sweet odor of earth rose from the valley under them, as she reached her hand up to him with the young dove.

"I'm nimble as a nannie-goat," she boasted. "Take it, Lem."

He held it awkwardly, and it struggled in his hand. His tall figure stood above the girl as she climbed up the moss-grown rock. Her head was thrown back against the sky and the valley that she had named *Beauty of Kaintuck*. Her eyes met his suddenly, and he thought, now I know them to be a living blue.

And it seemed he was young and he could move the Shoestring over, and the oak trees and tear the sky apart with ease. Dulcie felt it too, as she gained the mountaintop. When he reached for her, she drew back. He flung the half-grown nestling from him as he grasped the girl impatiently. He kissed her and heard the dove rise flapping above them, uttering a high piping. Then it was falling in a slow spiral, and Dulcie pulled away.

"I'm promised!" she cried.

"Come away with me, Dulcie!"

She leaned down to brush the moss and dust from her dress. Her hair, thrown forward, rushed to the ground like a running stream. She said briskly:

"I see there comes my sweetheart!"

"You hear me, Dulcie?" he insisted.

Children and Lovers

"I'm bound to Will Hamm there. He's undertaken to care for Jessemine too, when it's time."

The youth was shambling along the distant path. His coat was soiled, and his work boots muddied. All his clothes seemed somehow too small for the pillar of a boy he was. His eyes were deep-pitted and the large knuckles of his huge hands stood out. He shouted:

"Are you wasting the day a-wandering, Dulcie? There's a lot of work to be done!"

The girl was moving already toward him. Lem Adam whispered hoarsely after her:

"Dulcie! He'll wear you to a rag! I'd care for you!"

She turned around. He waited, for he thought he dreamed and she was but a figment of his mind. She took the moon calendar timepiece from her pocket and fingered the engraving of the stag. She opened the lid carefully.

"I see the moon's coming in the light tonight. I'll be studying out how to read this in the years to come." She laughed, and when she reached the side of Will Hamm, the two of them started toward the Tolliver cabin.

The man groped for his black satchel where he had laid it among the bushes. "Have mercy on me, O Lord! For I am weak. All the night make I my bed to swim, I water my couch with tears." That was a piece of a psalm he had read once.

He looked to where the couple had come to a bend in the path. Dulcie waved back to him. The birds began to sing steadily in the scented light. He stumbled down the mule path. At the foot of the Shoestring he turned left by the burial place where the graves had been robbed. An owl called softly and flapped out of one of the persimmon trees. He whispered:

"*Old Tom Walker under your hat. Father, Son and Holy Ghost,*" the way blue-eyed Dulcie would have done.

He knew Tom Walker was the name the country folks had for the devil. His long legs traveled on, and after a few miles he came to where the clay-eaters had hunted the hearth clay.

Witch Chicken

There were two of them now with a paper sack to share. He kept remembering the soft-winged taloned witch chicken swinging over the burial ground. As he strode now down the pike toward Four Valleys the jackass brayed, and there were ten miles more to go.

The Cord

"We'll kill him this morning."

Jonas woke from his dream, hearing his father's strong voice in the next room. He kept his half-opened eyes on the muslin curtains stirring in the March breeze.

"Wait until Jonas is gone," Mama said. "I don't want him to see anything."

Jonas closed his eyes. The damp soft wind blew, and Jonas felt the pulse begin to beat heavily in him.

"I told Stack last night to dig the hole first thing today," Father said. Stack was the hired hand, old and white-headed; he'd been around as long as Jonas could remember.

"Now you wait until Jonas has gone for his turtles," Mother worried.

Jonas lay without moving his cramped limbs. Today was Saturday and he didn't have to go to school; he hated second grade. He'd told them all at supper that he was going to the far pasture to find the spring-moving turtles that he collected. He kept them in a pen near the yard pump; every spring he got absorbed in them.

His father's voice went soft and he said, "Mama, how do you feel?"

"Fine. I think I've a little while to go yet."

Mama was going to have a baby any time, and every morning when Jonas left the house with his sisters to catch the school bus, they had to holler at him to hurry because he stopped to spit on the small gray stone he kept under the flagstone at the bottom of the back steps. He would rub his saliva on the smooth surface and as it turned dark he would whisper:

> *"As my spit makes my stone blue*
> *I'll wish a wish and it'll come true!"*

Jonas could hear his sisters now, and he sighed. They were eleven and twelve and slept at the end of the hall and Jonas spent a good deal of his time at war with them. Although he was seven last fall, he felt the addition of a baby brother would be a help in handling the pair of them. They were shrieking and giggling in the hall now. He hoped they'd wait to invade his room until his father finished talking.

"I'll chalk a cross on his temple and use the rifle. That's the cleanest way," Father said.

"Chief was a good plow horse when he was young. Father. Remember?"

"Of course I do, Mama. I traded for him right after we were married. I'd throw the harness on him and then I'd put you up on his back while we went out to the field."

Mother sighed, "I never had a worry in those days."

Outside a wren was chanting, *"Teakettle, teakettle, teakettle,"* because it was spring and the rains and winds were over for a while.

Nora and Grace were whispering outside Jonas' door, about whether he was awake or not, scuffling their sheeps-wool slippers. He hated them easily, holding his breath.

Father's voice was clear. "Stack's too stubborn, Mama. If he weren't so old, I'd turn him out. He's bullheaded too, being from the back country. And he wants to get rid of Chief the way they did in old-time days, when saving on gunpowder mattered. Stack figures he'd be doing us a favor. I told him I put my foot down and we wouldn't have any nonsense."

"Don't let him hurt Chief," Mama said.

Children and Lovers

"I'll be there to see it's done right. Don't you worry. I know you're fond of Chief. He's all crippled up or I'd pasture him here till he died a natural death."

"They say," Mama said, "that the longer you put off having a baby, the more likely it is to be a boy."

"I know," Father chuckled. "And I'm counting on it."

Then the girls were charging in upon Jonas, pitching themselves upon his bed, bouncing on the springs, Grace's long brown hair swinging, Nora's giggle high.

"We're going into town on our ponies!"

"Come too, Jonas!"

He shook his head, turning on his stomach, ducking under the pillow to shut out the sight and sound of them. The two tucked their blue flannel gowns that Mama had sewed for them around their legs. Nora had a sash around her waist because she thought her breasts were beginning to show, and she was pleased about it. She cried, "We'll buy you a cherry ice at the drugstore." She pulled the pillow away from Jonas' head.

Grace hadn't started to hope about breasts yet. She said, "And chewing gum too if you'll come with!" She flung her long hair forward and down over her face in her newest habit, which Jonas considered her most obnoxious. She shouted, "What's the difference between an elephant and a flea?"

Jonas declared, while his heart pounded steadily, as it had done since he'd first been awakened by the voices, "I'm going down to the far pasture like I said last night at supper."

"We're stopping in at the bird exhibit they've got in the hall of the Town Library too," Nora told him.

"And there's a display of turtles," Grace said, crafty, parting her hair and grinning.

"I won't."

In the fall when the hogs or a steer were butchered, Mama always sent Jonas and the girls away. Jonas had seen chickens die, when Mama ran down a couple of them for a meal, out in the yard. Mama laid a broomstick across their necks and pulled on their legs and their heads came off, and she threw them out in the yard to flop and bloody up their neck feathers, until they subsided in warm heaps. Then she set Jonas or the girls to plucking them.

Jonas stretched his limbs under the bedcovers, feeling the strong muscles of his small body. The horse, Chief, was so old he was more than three times Jonas' seven years. His arthritic legs creaked when he walked. Jonas and the girls had used to ride him out in the pasture sometimes, but he wasn't even safe for that any more. The last time they had caught Chief and, three astride, gone ambling along, the white horse had stumbled to his knees and sighed and lain down and they all slid off. They couldn't coax him up to his feet again for a long time. They told Father, who said they'd have to think about putting Chief to sleep one day soon.

Jonas understood that meant to die. He knew everything died in its time. Sometimes he felt sorry for Mama and Father because they were so much older than he was and had that much less time to live. Jonas counted his prospective years, a little fearful, but feeling safe because the blackness of his own death was so distant. Supposing he were Chief and it were today!

The girls got off his bed and Nora said, "He's getting hopeless, Grace. He never plays with us any more."

And Grace told Jonas, knowing he didn't care, "An elephant can have fleas but a flea can't have elephants." And they were gone, noisy.

Jonas put his hand to his temple and made a cross with his finger upon it. "Zowie," he whispered, feeling the bullet charge through the old white horse and the terror of the unknown descend.

His parents were going downstairs and the smell of frying bacon and perking coffee soon was drifting up the hallway, mixing with the scent of the spring wind. Jonas got up and pulled on his overalls. It was warm enough to go barefoot now, and he left his shoes where he'd tossed them when he came home from school the day before. He went down to the kitchen. Mother pulled him into her arms and hugged him. Jonas could feel the baby under her apron.

Mama said, "Good morning, Jonas!"

Jonas slipped away from her, "Good morning, Mama."

Mama watched him take his seat at the table. "All the turtles will be out marching over to the creek in the far pasture today."

She never said a word about what was going to really happen. Father nodded at Jonas, and he knew Father was just waiting for the three children to clear out. Jonas looked at Mother's stomach, as she moved about the room, half-clumsy with her burden, breathless sometimes. The baby was going to leave her body any day now, and that was the opposite of the white horse. Sometimes the baby would kick; Mama let Jonas feel it once when he came to sleep with Father and Mama in their bed, when he'd had a bad dream.

"Eat your bacon, Jonas," Mama urged.

But Jonas shook his head; he couldn't eat. He felt slightly sick as though there were a birthday today, perhaps even his, and he might receive some wonderful gift.

Mama thought he was excited about turtles. And so she put bacon and some eggs that she fried with their yolks broken, between slices of her dark home-baked bread. She wrapped the food in brown paper and slipped it in the pocket of his denim jacket. "Go along, Jonas. Stay out all day if you want. Isn't it too early for him to go barefoot?" She appealed to Father. "Make him put on his shoes!"

"Let him alone, Mama," Father said. "Our son's not a baby any more."

But her anxious eyes followed Jonas. "I want to see how many turtles you can find," she told him.

Jonas knew Mama was afraid he might get back too soon, and he assured her, "If there aren't any turtles out there, I'll hunt for snakes, Mama." And he pulled on his coat and went out the door. He passed the flagstone and returned to nudge it

The Cord

with his toe. For safety-sake, he dug out the gray stone and spit on it, whispering. He could hear them still in the kitchen.

"Can we feel the baby kick?" Grace was asking, and Jonas knew she had swung her hair over her face.

"Both of us hope it's a sister, Mama," Nora said.

"Whatever happens, you'll please somebody here," Father laughed.

"I thought I felt something then," Mama sighed to Father.

Jonas pushed the stone back under. He went down the lane and past the barns. He thought one of the family might be watching from the house, and he wanted them all to think he was gone and out of the way. As he rounded the clapboard shed at the lane's end, he saw Stack up at the top of the greening hill pasture, digging a great hole. Jonas stopped in his tracks and turned to slip into the shed. It was an old building, erected long before the farm was owned by Father. The uneven roof leaked; the rats had deserted the place as unprofitable; a few field mice lingered; a rusted hay rake was tipped over in a corner. Jonas scrambled up the rungs of the loft ladder.

The three children played in here now and then; the last time was in the fall. Grace and Nora reported to Mama afterwards how Jonas had made water in a pop bottle and lorded it over them because they couldn't. Mama had taken Jonas on her lap and had a long talk with him about courtesy. She hadn't told Father. Now Jonas examined the tiny spider-webbed open windows set in dormers on each side of the high-slanted roof, anxious to view the scene. But they faced in the wrong directions, and Jonas was afraid he would be spotted by Stack if he leaned out. He sat down to think over what he should do.

He heard the various noises without. In the paddock his spotted pony was neighing shrilly as his sisters led their two out to saddle them before heading for town. From the barns sounded a steady lowing as hay was pitched down to the cattle by Father and corn was doled into the troughs. Overhead in the oak tree, which distributed its acorns onto the shed's steep roof every fall, a brown thrasher endlessly repeated its liquid notes into the morning. From high in the sky, came a desultory minor-keyed honking as a late flock of Canada geese flapped northward.

Heavy boots were scuffling along the lane below. Jonas got to his knees to look from the window. Stack had his thumbs hooked in his overall suspenders, as he went to the barn, stocky, white-haired, his neck and arms thick. When he was out of sight, Jonas moved over to the other window and sat, restless, to wait for what might happen.

In a while there was a scratching at the sill, and Jonas turned his head to meet, eye to eye, a hurrying gray squirrel, which scampered away, along at the eaves and up over the roof, disappearing. At once Jonas slid his legs over the sill to follow, swinging himself out onto the roof. He scrambled along the eaves and disintegrating wood shingles until he found a position that suited him just below the roof's apex, where he was fairly well shielded from the sight of anyone who might go up to the hill pasture. He flattened himself against the sun-warmed roof, his feet supported by a jutting loosened clapboard. Acorns caught in the shingles rattled to the ground, disturbed. The sun in the blue sky bloomed over the pile of overturned black dirt in the field and the glinting shovel propped against the faraway fence.

Jonas leaned up on his elbow to get a sight of the barns and, in the distance, the house. He saw neither Father nor Stack nor Chief. He thought of the turtles out in the fields, wandering after mates, heading for the far pasture creek. Jonas liked to come upon them, lumps moving slowly; he tucked them inside his shirt and into his pockets. He'd fixed a pen for them, and he fed them toast and table scraps Mama saved, which they ate greedily. Jonas was beginning to think Father had changed his mind about shooting Chief today. He considered getting down

---

from his vantage spot and searching for turtles after all. He was a little afraid of the barefoot journey along the rotted roof and insecure eaves to the dormer window.

He heard the engine of the family Ford start up then, behind the house. When the car puttered into view down the drive, Jonas saw that Father was driving and Mama was beside him. That meant the baby had started to come and Father wouldn't have time to put Chief to sleep today. Jonas considered it, and felt a sudden edge of disappointment, as if he had been cheated and some promised gift had been withdrawn. He decided to make his way over to the dormer window. As he was backing down, the jutted shingle board under his bare toes broke and he began to slide. He grabbed for the rooftop, scratching his hands and knees on the rough wood, but holding his place.

He heard a sudden scrunch of shoes and hoofs below on the path. Over the edge of the shed he could see the white horse being led along by the old thick-bodied man. There was an axe too, with fresh-whetted shining blade. Jonas felt a quick start of terror and the pulse throb in his throat.

He held fast to the shingles that met at the top of the shed, not noticing the bruises on himself. His feet groped for and found another shaky board to support them. The old man and the beast were entering the pasture now. The one plodded before, tugging at the halter of the other stumbling after, shaggy mane and tail fluttering in the March air. Slowly they gained the hilltop. Once Chief nearly fell and Stack waited, leaning on the axe, until the beast stood steady again. It almost seemed the hired man's will made the lamed plow horse climb the steep and difficult way.

Jonas rested his chin on the rooftop. His footing was insecure, and he was afraid he might slip from the spot altogether. He thought, too, that Stack might turn and notice his head interrupting the line of the shed's roof. But Jonas felt he had to take the chance; he had to watch the blood; even Father had said his son was no more a baby.

The pair reached the heaped mound; they were silhouetted on top of the green field against the bright sky. The old man dropped his axe and tied the horse by his halter to a fence post. Then he went to stare into the hole he had made earlier. He seemed to be putting off what he had a fancy to do according to his ancestors' custom. Jonas held his breath, listening to his heart pound heavily against the warm crumbling wood beneath him.

Stack lifted the axe and sighted the horse behind the ear. He swung, and with the blunt end of the axe-head, struck. Chief staggered, pulling back against his halter, shaking his head, unfalling. Jonas heard his groan on the wind.

"Die," he whispered.

Stack ran his arm across his face and rested his axe on the ground a moment. He loosed the taut rope so the horse was untied. Chief lowered his head, swinging it back and forth, low to the ground. The man straightened and struck him as before with the blunt part of the axe-head, behind the ear.

"Die!" Jonas almost shouted it.

There was a moan and slowly as a falling tree, Chief started to go down. The old man, practiced at slaughter of cattle, caught the head back to tighten the jugular vein. He slit it with the sharp blade he had prepared. As the red spurted under his hands, Jonas pulled himself up onto the roof's axis. He rode it, astride, forgetting he might be seen.

Stack was busy with his chore. The horse, in a last burst of strength, was half-lifting the man off his feet as he rose, forelegs stretched stiffly, his blood gushing over Stack's overalls. The sun blazed brilliant and the noon hour came and went. On his side now, Chief struggled in his final throes. Then all movement stopped. The old man laid down his axe and undid the halter. He began to tug at the great body to get it over by the hole.

Jonas was scrambling back below the peak of the roof, concerned again that he might be seen. Stack never seemed to glance away from his work, maneuvering the carcass to where he finally tipped it in. Jonas, from where he lay against the shingles, could hear the man's labored breathing. Stack was reaching for the shovel then, and pitching the dirt back, covering Chief over.

The sun blazed. Stack pulled a red kerchief from his pocket and tied it about his head to keep the sweat from his eyes. After a long time, he was finished and was tamping the dirt down with the shovel-head in measured movements. He slung the halter over one arm and took the axe and shovel on his shoulder. With slow steps he was descending the hill. He was singing some old-time song in a rough low voice, as he passed below the shed-roof where Jonas was flattened. Stack's overalls were spattered and stained, his hands were smudged with earth, and the red cloth about his head was wet.

Jonas turned his body slightly to watch the figure going toward the barn. An acorn under him rolled down the roof and fell on the path. Stack glanced behind him, stopping his song. He squinted up at the shed, blinded by the sun, looking for a squirrel. He shrugged and resumed his tune, plodding away.

Jonas made his slow way back to the dormer window. He slipped inside and stood undecided. He felt he was about to cry and was worried for a moment. Then he remembered the bread and bacon and egg in his pocket. He tore off the wrappings and, sitting hunched under the cobwebs of the windows, ate, greedy. Leaving the crumbs and paper in the dust, he went to the loft ladder and, half-falling in his haste, his toes and fingers slipping over the worn rungs, descended.

Outside on the lane Jonas paused. He walked up the field side, hesitant. He went to the new heaped grave and stood on it. Then he stamped the new earth with his bare feet and they sank in deep. He began to run, full-speed, toward the far pasture. The air Jonas breathed was perfumed like clover. He felt his joy and that he could outdistance horse, man, squirrel, any beast! Instead of using the gates, he clambered headlong over fences in his way. When he became winded and it seemed he could go no further, he charged on, gasping, until his second wind came and he sped renewed.

Jonas knew he was immortal. He shouted, "Jonas! Jonas!" as loud as he could. Crows in a wood somewhere barked back at him, "Jonas!"

Only when he spotted a familiar small lump in the grass did he pause to scoop up the box turtle. He shoved it into his shirt, under the bib of his overalls. There, with claws tucked in, its hard shell bounced against Jonas' bare ribs where his heart beat strongly.

Even when he reached the far pasture he kept on running, round and round in huge circles, splashing through the creek and dashing up its banks. He couldn't remember later when it was that he finally had enough and dropped down in the warm long grass on the breast of a hill over the stream. There he reviewed in his mind the progression of events that was climaxed by the gushing blood as the cord of Chief's life was severed by the hired man's sharp blade.

When he came in for supper that night, the girls were preparing it, because Mama was at the hospital and the new baby was there too. Nora was stirring the soup. "It's a boy, and you should have come with us to town, Jonas."

Jonas shook his head and pulled his turtle out from his shirt. He sat in a chair and watched it put its head out first, curious, and then its legs. He patted the hard shell and thought how he would feed the creature soon. He rested one bare foot on the other. Jonas was tired and sleepy.

"After we left the Library," Grace said, and flung her hair in front of her face and looked through it at Jonas, "Nora bought a bra."

Nora was wearing blue jeans and a tight jersey sweater. "I needed one," she said, and turned the fire off under the soup.

"And we bought cherry ices at the drugstore." Grace took the hot potatoes from the oven with a folded dish towel and asked Jonas a riddle. "Why do people go to bed?"

The Cord

Jonas gazed at her without trying to answer. His turtle waved its legs in the air, cradled in his palm. He felt the slight burn of the scratches on his hands and arms and knees from the clapboard shingles of the shed roof.

Nora said, "Everybody knows that, Grace. Because the bed won't come to them."

And Father's boots were thudding up the back steps outside as he came in from the evening barn chores. The door slammed behind him. "Well, you got the brother you ordered, Jonas!" Father shouted, kicking his boots behind the stove, laughing.

Jonas told him, "I wished for him on my stone." He yawned and thought how some day he would tell his new brother all about today.

"What have you been doing, Jonas?" Father asked. "So I can tell Mama when I go to the hospital."

"Just say," Jonas said as he stroked his pet, "that I was out in the pasture finding my turtle."

Pouring the Wine

She stirred out of her dream, half-opening her eyes, and reached into the beach basket, feeling for her sunglasses. On the hot sand behind her a young sunbrown Italian crouched, elbows resting on knees. He hissed again, without moving his lips, his fingers interlaced. She put on her glasses, and raising on an elbow, turned to look at him. Then she dropped back onto the flimsy towel embroidered in red with the words: Albergo Grande di Venezia. Mary felt soothed, warmed, by the admiration of the nearby youth. Aware she had stayed overlong in the sun the past two days, she reached for the sand-gritted bottle of suntan oil, her fingers smoothing it over her arms, neck, face.

"Inglese? You speaka English?" The man had come to stand over her. She saw his ankles, a thin black band covering his loins. She shook her head. "Deutsch? Sprechen sie Deutsch? Español? Americano?" He sighed as she made no reply. Then he was walking away in the blaze of sun down the Lido's shore, from which, since it was the final strip of land toward the Adriatic Sea, the man's forebears had sailed the Venetian fleets in their conquest of the East.

Three years before, Mary had come to Italy, to Napoli, on vacation. She had taken a small passenger boat then, to a bathing place called Marechiaro that Italians frequented. She'd brought a bottle of birra in her beach bag. She'd felt the tremor of the moving boat, breathed in the water scent, and tasted the

79

bitter good beer. Boys swimming in the water along the way had smacked and kissed and yelled, "Bella bambina! Molto bella!" at Mary at the rail. At Marechiaro, she'd changed in the tiny wood compartment to her new bikini and gone to stand at the platform that overhung the Golfo di Napoli. The shore and the sea bottom below had been composed of crumbly volcanic rock. At her hotel in Napoli, from the balcony, she had seen Vesuvio lurking above the city, sometimes letting off a stench of sulphur like a burning match. Mary, at Marechiaro, idly watching the Italians diving in the green deep water, had heard the "*hsst,*" twice before she'd glanced over at the fair-haired, somewhat handsome, man. He'd been in Napoli on business from Milano. His name was Giancarlo, and he'd spoken almost no English, so that during the long week they'd spent together, they had relied almost entirely on Mary's midget English-Italian dictionary. Parting from Giancarlo back then had been like a physical wound to Mary, returning to her desk in Baltimore.

Whenever she'd felt, in the weeks that followed, the dream quality of the incident, she'd moved her fingers over a welted thin white scar on her upper arm. On the plane flying back to America, she had consoled herself that she would at least have a photograph for a souvenir, because they'd handed Mary's camera to a steward at the beach. He'd clicked the shutter while Giancarlo was laughing. But though the image of Mary had been perfectly clear, her dark glasses etched, her bikini bright, her kerchief tied to hold her blond hair from her face, Giancarlo had been a blur, his head thrown back to laugh. She'd torn up the snapshot. Of course they'd never corresponded, because Giancarlo was married; he'd even talked proudly to Mary of his schoolboy son.

She stood now, stretching. She'd come to Venice this year, not Naples, on purpose. She didn't want to disturb the old vanishing inner scar. A physical mark was different. She ran her hand over the white jagged line on her arm, which might never blend and disappear.

She pulled her bathing cap now over her hair, piled up in a
bun these days. She waded into the clear shallow laguna, diving,
skimming along the sand bottom. She returned to the shore and
gathering her towel and basket, changed into her sundress and
sandals. She boarded a bus and was delivered with its passengers
at the dock where the launch came and returned them to San
Marco. There, at the Square, Mary took a vaporetto and was
borne up the Canal Grande toward her pensione. Gondolas
passed, piled with cases of Coca-Cola or ten-gallon straw wine
bottles or travelers' trunks; sometimes tourists crouched in the
seats. The men guiding the boats were ruddy from the sun, their
flared pants dark, their over-blouses white, their shirts striped,
the pattern repeated all over the canals of the city.

Mary, on her way to a bench in the back of the vaporetto,
passed by an elderly Italian, who hissed the same as the man at
the beach and whispered, "Desidero!" Mary felt a lassitude, a
calm, as she took her seat. Everywhere in this land, turning
corners into piazzas or streets, entering churches, she came on
the nude idealized crumbling figures in marble, bronze, oil
paint, standing with grace and languid passion. In Baltimore,
where she managed the sales section of the Quality Office Supply, she had nearly forgot this.

At the Lista di Spagna, she left the vaporetto and went up
the street to the pensione. She crossed the vine-sheltered area
where tables were already laid with white cloths, a roll beside
each plate, the goblets turned over. The waiter, in his white
coat, bowed to Mary as she passed by. He was handing a napkin
to an Englishwoman, who had arrived at the hotel on the same
bus as Mary the day before yesterday, and was fingering her
pearls now, aroused. "But the flowers in Verona were not nearly
so nice as I thought they'd be. I noticed it!"

The waiter, imperturbable, said, "You have went on the tour
to the villas, Signora?"

"The bus took eleven hours to get there. I was so disappointed."

Pouring the Wine

"Tomorrow you try the Church of San Rocco, Signora. You like. There are many Tintorettos there. Is beautiful. You do what I tell you."

"And I take all the tours, too."

Mary went over the threshold into the lobby. The waiter continued to soothe the English tourist. "There are eight of the Tintoretto canvases, Signora. I think you like."

Mary was sure he had never seen them himself. He was as bland with the woman as he'd been with Mary on her arrival, telling her how lovely her neck was as he laid the napkin on Mary's lap.

In the dark anteroom, some new people were registering, a family of three, the fluent Italian speech spilling from the older man and woman. By them stood a black-haired young man, diffident, waiting for them to finish. He looked Mary up and down at once, intently, in the Italian manner.

Mary didn't heed him, because she was caught in a second of shock. She had recognized in the light-haired older man the profile of her former acquaintance in Naples, Giancarlo. Mary fumbled for her key on its hook and hurried up the narrow staircase, down the hall, along the dark-red worn carpet. She was remembering how the man had said, "Beautiful. Bella bambina," through the long nights of that week. Mary called it up deliberately, as she'd done many times back home, at her seat in her office, typing, telephoning.

In her room now she put on an orange silk dress she'd bought the day before in a Venice shop; it complemented her low-coiled blond hair and gray eyes. She slid her bare feet into white sandals. She put on pale lipstick, saw in the mirror the sunburn's tinge on her arms and face. She seemed to herself strange and alien, and somehow beautiful, standing in front of the tall double doors to the balcony. She had bought an American paper at the Piazza San Marco, and she carried it down to her table.

"Solo, Signorina?" a waiter asked. She nodded and followed him to a table with a single setting of silver and plate.

Another waiter was coming with a half-filled bottle of Soave, on which he'd pencilled Mary's room number the night before. "And what you want this evening, Signorina? You can have anything you like!" He shook out the great white napkin and laid it across her lap, brushing her breasts deliberately with his hand. "And where have you went today, Signorina?"

"To the beach. And I've forgot your name. I'm sorry."

"I tell you this morning. D'Agostino, Signorina."

"Will you pour the wine, D'Agostino?"

"In our country the women pour their own wine. They are not like the American women."

She didn't heed his murmuring voice, her eyes following the three guests taking their table across the room; Giancarlo's back was to her. "I've been away from Italy three years," she told D'Agostino.

"Why you wait so long to come back?" He poured the amber liquid.

"There are other places to see." Mary opened her *Herald Tribune* as he went away.

Giancarlo's voice, from their table, was half-recalled, as he ordered the dinner. Its tenor key, its timbre, were heard all over the hot country, the high-pitched persuasive Italian tones. His broad shoulders were half-familiar; his hair was longer; he threw his head back to laugh, in the same gesture that had ruined her snapshot. She put aside the newspaper, and over the wine glass and the plates of antipasto and later manicotti and then salad that D'Agostino kept bringing, Mary studied the trio. The woman was small; her dress was cut low and between her full breasts rested a studded medallion of La Madonna. Her hair, like that of the youth beside her, was blue-black; her forehead was wide, her nose strong and high—Florentine, Etruscan. One saw it in the portraits of the wives of Renaissance nobles in the

Uffizi Gallery. The young man had the same nose, his lips thin, his fingers long. His hair was brushed back and fell to his collar. He wore a loose sweater, the sleeves pushed up; his pants were tapered and tight-fitting, his black shoes pointed. He tapped his foot and in the soft tongue conversed with his parents. Their voices were musical and continual. Mary, at the Piazza San Marco in the morning, crumbling a roll for the pigeons, had heard a similar sound from the multitude of birds.

The young man looked over at her and nodded slightly. She dropped her eyes, cutting the pasta with her fork, able to eat only a little, playing with it, considering leaving the pensione and going on to Florence in the morning. He spoke of her to the others, for the woman glanced at Mary, a smile on her mouth. Then Giancarlo was turning. Mary hastily lifted her wine glass to hide her face, spilling a little. His features seemed austere, and the cut of his dark business suit made him appear elderly. He turned back to them abruptly, and she wondered if the movement meant he was startled. He'd given no sign of recognition.

D'Agostino was removing Mary's dishes. Then he brought a silver bowl of apricots, a peach, yellow-red plums, floating in water. "You take the peach, Signorina. Is best."

"No. I only want coffee, D'Agostino."

"Si. I bring you. But first you have the fruit, Signorina. Then I bring. Pronto."

Although annoyed at his persistence, she took the peach on her plate. She peeled it slowly with the knife, holding it with the fork. She was deciding to stay. The waiter hovered over her. She asked him, "Those Italians that have just arrived, they are from Milano?"

"Si, Signorina. How you guess? They come while their son makes a vacation for two-three days." D'Agostino added, "And if you wait till ten o'clock when I get off work, I show you something. I know Venezia. This where I was born. You like?"

"I can't, D'Agostino. I'm going to bed."

"This Venezia the most beautiful city in the world. I go to other places; I take a ship, and they say, D'Agostino, stay here and work for us. But I say, I got to go back to Venezia. You understand?"

"Yes."

"I think you no want to come with me because I work here." He stood over Mary, bending, smiling. She'd seen D'Agostino's features also, in some princeling wearing a red cloak in the galleria, and kneeling with others about La Madonna. The night concierge out in the hall too, in broad-striped cotton pants and skull cap, had the beak features of old Savonarola, burned more than four hundred and fifty years ago outside the Uffizi Gallery.

"No, that's not true."

"Is a good job," he assured her.

"I know!" Clumsy, she sliced the soft yellow fruit.

He held his ground, persuasive. "You want me to show you, just let me know. I wait for you. At the espresso bar across the bridge. You not be sorry."

Mary was aware that her eyes kept returning to the group of three who were laughing together now. She felt suddenly lonely. She rose. "Good night, D'Agostino."

He stood aside, and she fled past the desk where the concierge leaned on an elbow over an account book, up the narrow stairs. In the bedroom she went to the balcony. The water of the Canal Grande was just visible, down the street at the corner of the building, reflecting lights. She heard the faint singing of the gondoliers entertaining tourists as they plied them up the murky water and back at two hundred lira a round trip. A brown-frocked padre on a bicycle pedaled by. Far-off laughter was audible on the night air which had the scent of the canals on it. She thought back in time to Napoli and Giancarlo and how they had watched Vesuvio fade in the distance from the bedroom balcony three summers ago as night had come on.

There was a short rap at the door, and she turned to open it.

Pouring the Wine

D'Agostino had a small tray in his hands. "Your caffè. You forget, Signorina."

"But I didn't want it after all."

He slipped inside the door and closed it, putting the tray on the table. The white towel was on his arm. "Why have you went away so fast?"

"I'm tired, D'Agostino." Mary felt her voice sounded strained.

"First time I see you come here two days ago, I think, D'Agostino, she's twenty-five. You look so young."

"Please go." Mary began to laugh. "I'm almost forty."

He put his hand on her upper arm, over the old white scar. "Where you get this? When you are a child?"

Mary was tugging open the door. "Now, go!"

He slipped into the hall, bowing, formal. "Grazie, Signorina. Buona notte."

"Thank you for the coffee."

She turned to sit on the bed and pull off her sandals, at the moment wishing for her own country, for the hid prurience and the colder churches. Here daily she watched black-robed old women go down before a pocked sculptured madonna in the Basilica. There, over the centuries, the women's hands and mouths had worn the stone face away. Beads clinking, they were whispering all over Italy before representations of Christo Morto and the mourning Maria and the whirling angels.

At eight the next morning, Mary was on the gray carved steps below the Basilica, a little handbag and a roll from the pensione in her lap, a basket of swim clothes at her side. The clock tower above began to sound the hour; two metal blackamoors were beating the gong. At the first stroke, like a storm cloud, all the roosting pigeons flew about and then descended onto the pavement. Mary felt how all over Italy the same thing was happening in church piazzas. When the bell was still, the birds walked about, the males strutting, dipping, the females darting. "Coo-croooo, crrrrr-ooooo."

Children and Lovers

Mary broke her panino, and as she looked up, met the eyes of Giancarlo's son. He smiled, and Mary rose instantly, her bag falling to the stones. In a quick movement, he was retrieving it and was on one knee, his black eyes close to her, his handsome hawk nose. There was the soft statement, "Prego."

"Thank you."

"It is my pleasure, Signorina."

She hurried to escape, and he made no effort to stop her. She crossed rapidly over small bridges, went through winding ways and by shops and people, a green statue of a saint, a church official swinging past in long carmine robes. A student chirped at her, following for a few blocks, singing in a near-soprano, "Ti, ti, ti—amo!" She entered a church she'd never seen before. In all of them, in the painting hanging there of nobles or popes, were the mythical lions that dominated Venice, the symbol of Christianity, tearing horses under their claws, the symbol of evil. One of the lions stood winged on that pedestal in San Marco, his paw on the shield.

Mary was remembering Giancarlo again, back in Naples; how he'd known only a few words of English. His son seemed to speak it well enough. Her first dinner with Giancarlo had been at a restaurant high above Naples, the meal well served; they'd toasted each other, "Cin cin!" She'd told Giancarlo how people had warned her that Italian men never spent money on tourist girls. They'd walk them about the city, and buy them ice cream, gelato, at the stands. That was all. He had been amused and said it wasn't so. The next day he took Mary back to the bathing place where they had met, Marechiaro.

The sea bottom was rocky and deep, and Giancarlo had dared Mary to swim under water as far as the buoys. She'd plunged in, and as she went down, felt the slow painless slicing of her shoulder skin. She'd surfaced and climbed the ladder to show her bleeding wound. "It stings, Giancarlo!"

He'd laughed at her. "What a pretty arm, Maria! Si."

"But it hurts," she'd complained.

Pouring the Wine

"A beautiful arm. Questa bella." He'd kissed it above the blood.

"I suppose it's the custom of the country!" she'd said and dived into another spot carefully and raced him to the buoys. Later he'd called the attendant and instructed him to put alcohol on the place, and a piece of tape. Then they'd gone back to her hotel.

Finally, when they'd parted because her plane was leaving, Giancarlo had said, "I wish we no say goodbye. We say ciao, like we are meeting tomorrow."

Now Mary, standing in the Venetian church, wondered how long her mind had been turning upon time past. She left the building and wandered back to the square to cross to the Lido. There in her yellow bathing suit, she went to doze in the sand, in the unstirring heat, waking to listen to some unfamiliar bird warble. It would be in some gray-green tree whose name she did not know, with a knotted trunk, and the grass and the flowers underneath would be different from those in Baltimore. The sweat glided down her flesh under her suit, and she rose suddenly, running to the water, splashing through the blue, forgetting her cap, wetting her piled blond hair. She pulled out the pins and held them while she went under, swimming slowly along the bottom, her hair clouding about her head.

When she came up, she saw his face near her, his flashing smile. "We meet again!" He was lean and dark and young. "I am not following you, Signorina."

"I'm sure of that." Mary began swimming away in long strokes, half-pleased.

He called, "My name is Manlio. Would you like to take a boat?"

"No, grazie," she called back, panting slightly, swimming straight out and away from shore. She let the hair pins go in the water, to the bottom.

She felt his pursuit before she heard the splashes, effortless. Later, when they were far out, Manlio disappeared under for long seconds, returning with a handful of sand. "It's deep! Can you get some?"

She caught in her breath and struggled downward, scooping at the sea floor with her fingers, and shoving it with her feet to send her up quickly. She held out the grains. "Look!"

"Bene! Shall we go in to shore now?"

"I don't mind."

"The headwaiter told me your name is Mary."

"He's fresh!"

"What's fresh?"

"Like you. I wish I could stand on the bottom. I didn't know we were so far out."

He came close and put his hand to guide her fingers to his shoulder. "Hold on."

After a while, again in shallow water, they stood and waded toward the shore. Manlio pointed. "The boats are down there."

Mary found herself acquiescing. "Are we taking one?"

"Yes. And you have beautiful legs. Bella." Manlio walked ahead up the sand and spoke to the owner of the boats. Mary waited. And then he was pushing one out into the water and helping Mary to the bow seat. He rowed with long powerful movements. His skin was browned; a gold medallion glinted in the hair curls on his chest.

"What do you do, Manlio?" Mary combed through her wet hair with her fingers, indolent.

"Studente. In Milano."

"Of course." She felt his vitality; it almost tired her.

He moved continually, shifting his weight, talking, humming. "You like Perry Como, Mary?" The dark cloth over his loins was laced at the hips at each side.

"I think so."

"You like 'Scusi mi'?" He began to sing the tune, tapping his foot.

She glanced back at the Lido shore which was now a thin blue line. The boat was slowing. She was wary. "Manlio?"

"You want to swim, Mary?" He was putting up the oars, smiling, his teeth white.

"It's too deep."

"I will stay in the boat," he assured her.

Her movements in the sun were slowed as she rose and poised to dive. She felt like Michelangelo's Aurora rising from a marble sleep, the body exaggerated in its beauty, the legs elongated, the breasts near perfect. Her lone form went into the clear depths, her light hair streaming up. She tried to get a handful of sand from the bottom, and the fact that she wasn't successful made her almost afraid. She surfaced, gasping. She swam back to the boat, her laughter high, so the man recognized her fear.

"Come in now, Mary," he coaxed. But she would not and dove under again and again.

When at last she consented, he helped her over the boat edge, his lean fingers sinking into the soft flesh of her arms. He rubbed her with his towel, and even her salt-wet hair, diligent. Then he sprawled half-sleeping across the stern seat. "You want to siesta, Mary?"

"All right."

He'd been waiting for her to say it, and got up and shook the wet towel out in the sun. He spread it over the seat for her to lie across, smoothing out all the folds. She lay along the board, her head resting on the boat edge, her feet in the water. After a while Manlio was kneeling by her.

"I like your hair."

"Why?"

"Questa bella." He put his hand on the tangled hanging strands. He touched her half-shut eyes, her shoulder and the arm, over the scar from the rock in Napoli. "Bella." And her elbow and inner arm and her wrist. His mouth was on her fingers and on her knees, on her ankles. He was slipping down the straps of the yellow suit, and touching her sun-warm skin. "Desidero."

Children and Lovers

She stumbled over his name, having almost forgot it, "Manlio." The sea air was cool and they were alone in the center of the world.

"Stay there, Mary, so I can look at you." She felt as if she were one of the polished marble figures she saw everywhere, a piece of ancient Italy. And the sun was falling steadily toward evening. She was lying on the boat's floor, guarded by the towel, the gold medallion against her.

Then it was time to go and Manlio was taking up the oars again. He was singing while rowing the long way in. "Ti, ti, ti—amo! You like Frankie Sinatra, Mary?" His bare foot beat the time; his body swung to the effort; his long fingers held the weatherworn oars.

The shore was deserted, and Manlio had to hunt for the keeper of the boats to pay him. Mary waited, seated on an overturned hull.

When he came back, he said, "You still here? I thought you'd be changed by now."

She had forgot that Italian men were used to women who poured their own wine. "I'll go find my cabina."

"I'll be waiting here for you."

Before she rejoined him, Mary fumbled with her long hair, braiding it down her back, where it lay wet against her dress. She felt some regret by now, fastening her dress belt.

He put his arm about her, familiar. "Tonight I'll show you Venice."

Back at the Albergo Grande, Mary had a moment of panic, fearing they might meet Giancarlo. At the foot of the dark steps, Manlio said, "At ten you go to the espresso bar across the bridge and wait. My mama does not approve of American women for me, though she thinks you are beautiful. She said it last night."

Mary flushed. "What does your father think?"

"He says you are too old for me." Manlio's white smile flashed.

She ran up the stairs, without answering his call after her. In her room she went to the balcony before changing her dress. Standing in the tall windows, she listened to the crashing of the dishes and silver underneath and the calls of the waiters, their snatches of modern songs, "Scusi mi, Signorina!" Across the street one of the city's eagle-nosed beggar women whined in her long red dress, her uncrying infant thrust toward the tourists. "Bambino! Bread. Fame." Mary hung her bathing suit to dry on the door handle. She rinsed the salt water from her hair and toweled it and wound it in a low coil. She slipped into white jeans and a soft purple sweater.

She came down to the vine-hung dining area. The Milanese family were at their table, and the Englishwoman at hers, in her precise voice complaining to D'Agostino, twisting at her strand of pearls. "And who do you think the statue was? That awful San Sebastian again with an arrow through his neck!"

"Solo?" said a waiter to Mary.

She took her seat, still glimpsing out in the street the red skirt of the beggar beyond the tables. The white-coated D'Agostino was beside her. "You been taking the sun, Signorina?"

"Why don't you ever call me Signora, D'Agostino?"

"You look like a young girl." He flattered, unperturbed. "And have you went to the Lido?"

"Why?"

He gave her the menu card. "And have you went alone?"

"Yes."

"I think you not alone. I think you meet somebody there. I think so. And how many more days you got here at the albergo?"

"Two. But why do you say I met someone, D'Agostino?"

"When you let me show you Venezia?" He unfolded the napkin and spread it for her, touching her, practiced. "And what you going to have tonight? You think you like the fish? Is a nice trota. Or you like the lasagna?"

"Maybe the trout."

Children and Lovers

"No. The lasagna very nice this evening. You take it. Is good."

"All right."

"That's what I have before I come on here to work tonight. I have a plate of it. Very nice. And you start with the fish soup. And after the legumes. And cheese if you want. And fruit. You like the frutta or the ice cream?"

"The fruit."

He was going to the kitchen, calling, "For the signorina. Pronto!"

Manlio was speaking to his parents of Mary, because his mother's head was turning her way. Giancarlo in a moment looked over too, nodding, half-rising, formal. He reddened, and she savored his confusion, knowing he must recognize her now. Then his back was to her once more. She wondered what Manlio had said, and if they knew he'd asked Mary to meet him later. D'Agostino was uncorking a straw-decked bottle of red Chianti and pouring it, the common wine of Florence.

"You hear what I say, Signorina? I been in San Francisco one time. In America."

"Were you?"

"I work the bar in a ship stopped there." But all Mary could do was smile, and D'Agostino sighed and went away for her soup.

Mary lingered over her meal. Just as the trio across the room rose to leave, D'Agostino brought a silver tray of cheeses for Mary. "Which shall I take?" she asked him.

"The Gorgonzola, Signorina."

Giancarlo, who had been following his wife and son, turned and came over to Mary. His family went ahead and waited for him at the door. Giancarlo bowed, grave. "Buona sera, Signora."

"Buona sera, Signore."

He was speaking in rapid Italian to D'Agostino, who said, "The Signore wish you to understand he would ask you to join his family at their table but they speak very bad English."

"Grazie, Signore," Mary told Giancarlo. She felt the fading of the old wound, finally.

Giancarlo was bowing again. He gestured and said something else in Italian to the waiter. "Buona sera, Signora." He went to join his family and they passed into the anteroom.

D'Agostino said to Mary, "He recommends you try the Brie. Tonight is better than the Gorgonzola, the Signore says."

"Is it, D'Agostino?"

"I think maybe he is right, Signorina."

"I will have a little of each."

When Mary left, she was the last tourist among the empty tables. She went through the lobby up to her darkened balcony, waiting for ten o'clock when she would go to sit in the coffee bar across the bridge. In time Manlio would come and lean over and put her hand to his mouth and praise her. They would walk about the city. "I will show you beautiful dying Venice at night, Mary. And later buy gelato at the Rialto Bridge, if you want some." They would gaze into the canals where lone crippled gondolas were sometimes moored to giant iron rings, and where litter floated in the dark water. And he would come back with her to her room. And the Venetians below—the waiters, the stripe-suited porter, the concierge—knowing in some way, would approve.

And it happened that way. And then in the morning Mary, who must take a plane for America in one more day, was photographing the kitchen staff and the waiters. They came to the sunny arbored entrance-way, singing, posing. Mary even snapped the Englishwoman at her breakfast tea, so she would have an excuse to take a photo of the three from Milano, as well. The Englishwoman's hands tugged at her pearls, fierce; Mary took down her address and promised to send the picture. Manlio looked over at her and smiled gaily. His parents were discussing something in their quick tongue, and they stopped to nod to Mary, too. The trio were drinking their caffè e latte and spreading butter thickly on the gray crusty bread. Mary felt their hurry. Manlio's white teeth dug at the panino, and he was laughing as she took their picture.

As Manlio passed Mary, following his parents into the lobby, he pressed his hand on her arm. She felt Manlio must surely leave a souvenir, or at least say some final message to her, as he went away. D'Agostino brought caffè, and Mary waited, her camera on the table before her beside the *Herald Tribune*, the headlines of which she was reading repetitively. She'd sensed Manlio's detachment, his mind turning on whatever waited back in Milano. Giancarlo's tenor voice was raised, calling to the porter, who hustled up, trundling a two-wheeled baggage carrier.

Then the Englishwoman was taking the chair across from Mary at the table. "I'm waiting for the tour, Miss. We're doing a roundabout to the churches today." The pearls were wound on her fierce finger. "Do you take the tours?"

"Not often." Mary felt her disappointment, knowing Manlio couldn't stop and speak before a stranger.

"Yesterday they wouldn't let me into a cell in the monastery. I crawled under the ropes!" And then the woman gave a little cry, gasping as the pale drops broke apart and rolled down and clattered.

Manlio came striding out, pausing before Mary, restless, smiling. "Bye-bye, Signorina."

Mary nodded; unhappy. And his mother was there then, speaking softly to Mary, something in Italian that she couldn't understand. She took her son's arm and they went on. Then there was Giancarlo, bending formally over her hand, leaving a tiny package in it, murmuring, "Ciao, Maria."

"Ciao, Signore," she said, gazing after him.

The three figures were going around the corner after the porter, Manlio singing, "Ti, ti, ti!"

Another pearl fell and another from the Englishwoman's clothes and she bent stiffly to pick them up. A waiter came to help, and Mary watched the pair, the one exclaiming and the other pacifying. Mary felt the bruise on her neck from the rough boat seat a day ago; she would wait for it to heal and pass. She put the small package in her purse.

She got up and went out and down the street to the dock to take a vaporetto for Piazza San Marco. She sat in the café at one side of the square, and while she waited for the caffè and panino, discovered in the pink cotton, a gold St. Christopher medal, a traveler's charm. She hung it around her neck. When the bread came, she crumbled some on the rough stones for the rushing pigeons, ignoring the hoarse voice over her, the black eyes that looked down between her breasts where the small souvenir lay. "Solo? Speaka Inglese?"

That evening D'Agostino brought her camera to her table that she had forgot at breakfast. "You leave this, Signorina. You be more careful."

"Grazie, D'Agostino."

He produced the menu. "Tonight I think you have some meat. I think you sad, Signorina."

"No."

"The steak is very good for this. You have what I tell you tonight."

"I'm not hungry."

"You listen. You start with the spaghetti. And you have the steak Bismark, with the eggs up. You like that? You can have the insalata if you wish too. Is good with meat. You like that?"

"Si."

"And you have a nice wine, Bardolino, that's a northern wine, up by Garda Lake. Is good." He bent over her, solicitous.

"It's true, D'Agostino." She was surprised. "I am hungry."

"Food is the best for sadness. Is good." He returned and with quick movements of the corkscrew freed the foil and popped the cork. He sniffed it and swung his fold-creased white napkin about the bottle and poured.

She objected. "Let me pour my own."

"No. I do for you. The American women are different."

"Why do you say that, D'Agostino? They aren't."

"And you eat all I bring you this evening." He was gone, calling, "Pronto, pronto!"

When she lifted the glass a few drops spilled on the white cloth, staining it the color of the blood of that One celebrated all over this hot land, He who'd caused all the commotion in the great paintings.

Before she went up to her balcony, Mary, fingering the replica of the sturdy one-time saint she now wore, spoke to the Italian standing beside her, removing the bowl of fruit. "I'll have caffè in my room tonight, D'Agostino, I think."

He nodded. "Si, Signorina." He held her chair ceremoniously as she got up, the folds of her scarlet dress rippling in the shadow. "You got a beautiful neck, Signorina. Bella. You wait. After a while I come."

Pouring the Wine

Blue Neckerchief

Clate could have mislaid the neckerchief but right away he laid the blame on Maud. Clate was yellow haired, with a mouth so broad it took up most of his face. When he smiled, folks would melt like butter in the sun and do their best to keep him laughing. But when he was put out as with Maud now, he was fierce. "A wife," he scowled, "should know how each article, be it so small, is placed in her household!" She could not reply because of the sharpness of her own anger. She was afraid of what she might say.

Clate was going to the town of Faulie today, twenty miles off at the base of the next mountain. He wanted the blue kerchief to take up the wetness on his neck if it got hot and to pull up over his nose when a tourist's automobile would race by him on the road, roiling the dust. Clate was going alone on Whitey for Maud was four months along with a child. He went chiefly to buy new plow tips, but he would pick up bacon and sugar, too. And she had given him the list of seeds she wanted for her flower garden.

Clate's last tip had cracked yesterday. Maud had been listening to him in the hillfield below the cabin, while she was redding up her housework. He sang to drive his young work horse, different tunes he had learned as a child from the old men. He didn't note the words, which were often quaint, but roared strongly so she had to smile. And then he shouted, "Gee-ho, there, Whitey!" Maud herself couldn't carry a tune, but she did relish her husband's voice that was true as a bird's. Suddenly the song had cut off, and when she walked out to see the trouble, Clate called from the field that the steel piece on the plow had split on hitting a rock, and he was bringing the horse in.

Now he was riding off, bare necked, his big mouth sullen, down the path, his legs dangling beside the stirrupless old saddle. He would not look back to his young wife pouting in the doorway. The sky, shed of dawn, was of the blueness of wild iris. She turned from it and from the sounds and scents of spring into the cabin's dusky interior, lit by one window. She shook out the blankets and straightened the bed. Over the fireplace gleamed a brilliant painting that her husband had bought from a passing salesman. That was when Clate had first made up his mind to ask Maud to wed, though she was only sixteen; and to come to this single-room house on his piece of ground. The colors had been brushed on the black velvet; a phoenix-bird, golden and red, flying up alive from the grave fire it had made for itself. Her eyes glanced over it familiarly in the same way she saw the rock chimney chinked with rose-red mortar, or the low German spinning wheel that turned with a foot pedal, or the new loom filling the corner.

Maud stood in the spring-scented room and thought of her mother, who was tall and soft-breasted, gay. Maud was not used yet to Clate's moods! They were married now a little more than a year. In her family had been a father, steady and thoughtful, and six sisters wearing down the threshold with dashing in and out. If any of them quarreled, it was careless, passing easily. But with Clate, who was ten years older, who thought and spoke faster than she, it was as if their every disagreement were of great moment. His voice had been loud, crying, "You ought to know where you folded it away!"

She brushed her tears with her arm in a gesture of inade-quacy. Since she'd known of the baby's coming, she would weep easily from any emotion. She went to the hearth to rake back the coals, and the gray-blue smoke over the cabin wreathed and thinned and ceased. She filled the coal-oil lamps on the table and mantel. She thought of how her husband would please himself in the town. He would stop in the store and buy a handful of black rolled cigars. He would stand on the corner, his yellow hair slicked down, and smoke one, while thin town girls in their bright dresses went by. She turned her jealousy over in her, feeling it tenderly as it overlaid her fading anger; a lump of pity came in her chest. She went out the door to open the gate so the flock of chickens could scatter to hunt bugs and wild seeds. One blue hen was penned apart with three goslings she had hatched out from a clutch of giant cream-colored eggs. While Maud fed her wet meal, the hen clucked in a brash triumphant way, her feathers fluffed, the meat worn from her bones with the long waiting.

The sunlight was braiding into the various wild bird calls and into the unmoving violet mist that shrouded the mountain crouching across from this one. The town of Faulie knelt at its feet, concealed from Maud by the low hills and forest between. The brown banty rooster scuffled for purchase on one of the old seed hens. Releasing her, he fluttered his wings and squeaked shrill. Maud turned back to the cabin. Here she was standing in a sulk, and there was a day's work before her!

She spun well as did all her sisters. And they wove with care, seldom making mistakes. She would buy for her baby from what she got for the bedcover started on the loom now. She would sell it to the tourist-trader when he came in July. She was using the summer-and-winter weave, laying the pattern threads tight, without skips, so the design would emerge white on blue ground on one side; on the reverse, blue on white. Her father, proud of all his daughters' skill, had made a hand-shuttle loom for each one so far, before her wedding. Needing more of the stout linen thread, Maud sat at the stool. The flax was twirled and drawn with her steady hand; her small foot was judicious on the pedal.

While she was occupied there, over the lisp of the little wheel, a far-off drumming touched the air. She stopped the machine, lifting her head and waiting until the sound ceased. Then she put her thread down and stood. The pheasant was back! She left her work, stepping into the yard, crossing the spongy earth of the side field Clate had plowed yesterday. She was hurrying beneath orchard trees where the plums still sprinkled white blooms. The fragrance was overpowering, and very like the green grape blossoms' scent in early summer. She halted once at a rail fence to catch her breath, and to listen for the sound yet on the hill beyond. She climbed the fence, quick, afraid the bird would be flown before ever she could get there! Her mother had told them as little girls that a grouse pounded with his strong wings on the log to make that noise. It was the way he summoned his harem each year at this time. But Maud's mother had never seen the bird. She told them stories about his shyness. He might be fabled, not real. He could be a ghost bird, for if you tried to slip up on one, following the muted thunder, he vanished. But Clate said that was because the bird was able to throw his drumming where he pleased, from one hill to the next. She was nearing the racket, moving slow.

She stopped behind a tree and peered around the trunk. The rolling had subsided abruptly. A small brownish speckled bird cocked his head, motionless, mounted on a bone-smooth fallen tree. Decaying feathers were strewn from other years on the ground about. As if conscious perhaps of a watching she-grouse's eyes, he strutted a few steps. Then he stopped and ruffed his black neck feathers like a cape and spread his tail high. He bobbed his head like a banty-cock about to crow, and was bracing his feet, protruding his chest. His wings came out like graceful drooped fans and he swung them back and forth. Faster and faster! A measured hollow boom was audible as the

---

Blue Neckerchief

air was trapped in his lashing wings. The sound mounted furious to a crescendo. The bird-shape was dissolved in the flurry of feathers.

Maud was leaning her cheek on the tree. It was a hornbeam; the bark had a bluish cast; her grandsire's grandsire had chosen such a tree for his ax handles and for the beams, the part of the oxen yoke that went across the horns of the beasts and took the greatest strain. The grouse all at once desisted. His feathers fell into place, his wings folded, his tail lowered and flattened. He seemed shrunken. He tucked his beak to his feet, wiping with two quick sidewise movements. He began to walk his log again, in a subdued fashion.

Maud saw the weasel that wound, sliding, toward the center of the clearing where the bird moved. She pushed the hornbeam tree from her; the brush crackled beneath her hasty foot. Instantly the two buttons of the long dark creature were fixed startled on her. Then in several silent gliding leaps it disappeared. The grouse was whirring away, blending into green shadowy branches. Maud bent to pick up a long feather that fluttered. The heavy musk of the frightened weasel was apparent. No sound had come from any of the three except for the breaking twigs.

She turned to make her way homeward; she again climbed the rail fence and swung down the other side. In the cabin she got a glass jar and placed the glossy feather like a flower in it, and set it on the table. Her eyes wandered about the room, still somehow hunting for Clate's blue kerchief. She went over to her low stool and started the wheel. The flax seemed alive and ran and twisted through her fingers. After a while when the spindle was half full, the sun climbed over the door sill as it traveled down the west sky.

One day she would be old in this house! Sons and daughters would rise tall as saplings about her. That pheasant would return each spring to dance on his worn log in the middle of his feather-carpeted stage. And she would have learned the ways of her husband and how to please him. She would plant and tend her gardens. This year's flowers would be all of yellow, with town-bought seeds and day lilies and sunflowers. The idea pleased her. Another year maybe all of blue; cornflowers and asters, and wood-sprung violets and flags she would dig. She was humming one of Clate's songs in her off-key:

> If I had but known before I courted
> That love had been so hard on me;
> I'd have fastened my heart in a box of golden
> And locked it up with a silver pin!

The log walls and joists and the split floor of chestnut and hickory that surrounded her were so smooth that one might think them sawed and planed. Clate was clever with a broadax and drawing knife!

The rug of sunlight just reached her agile fingers when Whitey's hoof-step came. She heard Clate speaking and she sprang up. He was striding in the doorway. He was taking the sun to him so he stood there of golden! His eyes even were soft gold. His mouth that some called ugly was gold, too. She was blinded, feeling the silkish scarf he was putting into her hand from the dime store in Faulie. He began relating what had happened, waving his arms. He had watched an accident. Two cars crashing on the side of the mountain over Faulie! He had seen them against the sky like little rearing bugs, as he was reaching the town on Whitey. The two black beetles had been approaching each other in a puff of dust, and then soundless were tumbling over the ripped-wood guard fence. All Faulie had been buzzing with it!

Wide-eyed, she cried, "What if it was you, Clate?"

But his mouth split into a laugh. "I got you a little kerchief and I had it to deliver, didn't I?" He was pulling out a chair and sitting at the table.

She thought how she had planned the years of her life while he had watched that thing happen. "The pheasant was drumming today," she said.

"I heard him too, Maud."

"Wonder if those folks in the cars did." She blinked her easy tears. "And if they knew what it was."

"They were tourists," he said, careless.

She held the cloth he had given her in the sunlight. It was like blue creek water. "It's pretty."

"I thought you'd like it, Maud."

Then she remembered, "Say, I recall where I put that neckerchief! It's in the chest."

"What neckerchief?" He played with the feather with his finger, idle, content to be at home with this small woman again.

"The one this morning!"

"I had forgot." He was drawing her to his lap. "Those town girls are real spindle-shanked." The cigar odor was on his breath. Gold was shining from the flaming painted velvet over the fireplace and from the opalescent single feather, and in the man's golden soft eyes.

The Other One

After Clive Christy had sent the wire, he waited from Saturday until Wednesday, pacing up and down in his efficiency in the glass-walled apartment house in Washington, D.C., until it dawned on him that Danielson must have thrown it into the round file under some hotel table. Danielson probably abhored disciples and the stuffy telegram made him sound like one: IMPERATIVE I MEET YOU WILL YOU CONSENT REPLY COLLECT RESPECTFULLY.

He blamed himself for a wrong move and sat down on the sleep bed to draft a letter, addressing it to the University of St. Jude, where the famous poet was to live for the next eight or nine months, as Artist-in-Residence. Clive explained that he was thirty-four, a freelance writer, also a pretty competent photographer. He'd memorized "The Asgard Wall," when he was a high school freshman. (He thought the poet'd like that even if he was sick of hearing it.) He said since then he'd read every one of his books as they came out of Minnesota where Bjorn Danielson was born and made his name, and later from Sweden where he'd gone into voluntary exile to get away from the "harassments and artificiality of American life," to quote his own words. Christy was asking permission to come and live nearby for the next few weeks, observing and photographing the master at work as well as in repose with his family about him. He wanted to do a biography and had a publisher inter-

105

ested. Of course there had been many articles and even one book published on the poet. The latter, *The Chain of Gleipner*, he'd found a confused and soppy eulogy, but he didn't put that in the letter.

Within a few days there was a reply, typewritten, brief, initialed *BD*, inviting Clive Christy to be a member of the Danielson household until he gained the material he needed. At once he packed his grips and assembled the camera equipment, golf clubs (he'd read that the master enjoyed golf) and his Olivetti. He loaded them into the five-year-old Fiat and told the girl at the desk to forward any mail. It took seven hours to get there, counting a stop to fill up the tank and buy cigarettes and peanut butter crackers. It was after five when he rapped at the door of the house, which was large and plain, and hard to find. A young woman opened the door, the hall behind her dark and cluttered.

"You must be the one Fader mentioned. Come in and I'll tell him you've arrived." Tall, freckled, cool-eyed, with reddish-blond hair cut short, she was wearing a wool skirt and sweater, a golden cross at her throat. She smiled slightly.

"Thanks."

A lanky Russian wolfhound dashed up. "Don't pay Loki any mind. He's spoiled." She laughed as the beast hurled himself up on Christy's lapels. "Now, Loki."

She disappeared. He knew Loki was the demon, the villain of Norse fairytales. Danielson's work was founded upon Scandinavian mythology. He pushed the dog down, looking around at the confusion of boxes piled about, the barrelful of walking sticks, the set of green battered file cases. Since after all he was there for that, he pulled open a drawer. It was banked with folders of news clips. A girl's voice spoke behind him.

"Hallo."

He slid the drawer shut slowly, turning. "Are you Freya?" (In *Who's Who* he'd ascertained that the daughters were twenty-seven and thirty-one.)

"Nej, I'm Lara." He understood her to say *nay* until he realized it was the Swedish *no*. "You're Mr. Christy." She put out her hand and then slipped it away, kneeling to pat the dog. "Don't be surprised if Fader puts you to work on some of those." She motioned to the files. She was much like her sister, except her hair was lighter and combed back in a chignon and she wasn't as pretty.

"On those papers? Wonderful."

"Does he know you're here?"

"Your sister went to tell him."

And then the old man was coming down the hall. He was portly and limped because of gout and always carried a cane. "Come to the drawing room, Mr. Christy." He put his arm about Lara. "And min dotter will bring us some litet bröd and some of the fine paste that she and her mother put in a bowl." He waved his hand. "Ask no questions and they'll tell no lies." The girl went away. "Like a drink?"

"Yes, sir."

Danielson went to the sideboard where bottles and a pitcher of water were standing. There was ice in the container. He fumbled about with the glasses and poured carefully, handed one to his guest, half-full. He raised his eyebrows explaining, "Have to watch that stuff. Like the old woman that wrestled Thor and overcame him."

"Ah, but that hag was Elli, Old Age." Clive was glad he could remember that much and that he'd discovered his tongue.

"*Old Age and Drink go hand in hand.*" Danielson took a taste from his brimming glass and set it on the table by him. "That reminds me of a story. A man was visiting England and he went into a pub to order a stout. Now, how did that one go?" He thought a moment before dismissing it. "Oh well, what's your background?"

Christy nursed his weak drink along, telling about a prize he'd got in journalism some years before and about his steady difficult rise since then. "I feel this will be a book you'll be pleased with, Mr. Danielson. It's the sort of work I enjoy doing."

"There are some papers I'll give you to look over tonight, Mr. Christy." He smiled at Lara, who was bringing in a little wooden tray of flatbread and a dish of something creamy and orange. "Well, what's this?"

She offered it to him and he used his left outspread palm for a plate, dipping the crackers and laying a series of them on it. "Ask no questions, Fader." She laughed, indulgent. "Want your sweater? It's chilly."

"That would be good."

She put the tray down by him and left. He motioned Clive to it while he bit into his food. Christy got up and helped himself. "Caviar." He tried to control his hunger.

"That what it is?"

Then an elderly woman entered the room, carrying a sweater, her black hair apparently dyed, her face gentle and wrinkled. This was Astrid, his little star. The poem Danielson had written about her and her "blue-black, river-black hair" had been translated into eleven languages that Christy knew of. Bonjour, Astrid! God dag, Astrid! Buenos dias, Astrid! Gut tag, Astrid! Hello, Astrid! In Chinese, Russian too. Christy got up quickly. She shook his hand and said pleasantly, "Perhaps you'd like to bring your bags up, before it's too dark, and let me show you your room?"

"Of course."

"Sit down," Danielson said. "No hurry. You visit with me and later when I'm taking my nap before dinner, you can do that."

She agreed. "Is that all right? You don't mind?"

"No indeed! I'm so overwhelmed by all of you. This is so rare a favor."

The dog trotted in and sat by Danielson, who spread a cracker and set it on the rug before the animal. Mrs. Danielson looked at them reproachfully. "Loki, how spoiled you are."

Children and Lovers

"I'll be writing my memoirs soon, Mr. Christy. As soon as this epic trilogy is done." He rubbed his gouty leg. "My publishers are already asking about it."

"They don't mind me doing this book?"

"No, no. There was a stupid fellow did another biography a few years ago. What was the name of it? Ever hear of it?"

"*The Chain of Gleipner.*"

"Ja." He said *yaw* in a heavy deliberate way. "Couldn't put up with him for very long. He even stole that title from me. Know what the chain was used for, Mr. Christy? Let's see how much you know of mythology."

"Something about a wolf, wasn't it? Who was Loki's son."

"Yes, the gods bound him with the Gleipner chain. It was forged of the noise made by the footfall of a cat, and the beards of women, the roots of stones, the breath of fishes and the spit of birds." He fixed another tidbit for the wolfhound. "And that fellow was a sneak of the first order! Took a few items of value from my papers. I made a list which I'll use someday. Lots of things I never told him about myself. I may let you in on a few secrets. Here's one: my name wasn't always Danielson."

"No?"

"It was Drang. But when I decided to write seriously, I saw that Bjorn Drang sounded like an old church bell." He wagged his head. "Bjorn Drang!"

Clive was beginning to feel as if he'd come on a diamond mine. He found it a strain to keep his eyes from the table of bottles near the doorway. He wanted to celebrate. "It's fascinating!" He smiled at Mrs. Danielson. "Never ran across that fact."

"No one knows it." Danielson got up and moved across the room, grunting as if in pain. His wife and Christy came hurrying to help. "Nej! Do it myself. Those papers are in here." He bent over a desk and lifted out an armful of folders. "Take your time on them. We'll put in an hour or two tomorrow afternoon together. Now, you must ask Mrs. Danielson questions too.

The Other One

She's a poet, you know. Ja. Now I'll have my little nap." He was gone, the dog padding after.

Christy turned to Mrs. Danielson. "I've run out of adjectives! Magnificent. He's wonderful. I don't know what I expected. Somebody dour, I suppose, egg-headed, sacrosanct, sacred?"

"You might like to freshen that drink. And then perhaps you should see your room. We eat at seven."

At a few minutes before the hour, Clive came down the stairs. His room was up yet another set of steps under the rafters. The family had gathered in the lighted drawing room, a blond girl of three perhaps, wearing pink robe and slippers, stood before Bjorn Danielson reciting some rhyme. Christy was surprised, not knowing there was a baby. Danielson hailed him. "Here you are, Mr. Christy. This is my littlest dotter, Fröken Squiggle."

The child squealed and threw herself on his leg. "Nej! Nej! Fader!"

Freya got up smiling. "She'll never be able to sleep. Come, Bruna, make a curtsey to Mr. Christy and shake his hand." The child bobbed quickly and ran up the stairs.

By the time everyone was seated around the table, Freya was back, sitting beside Lara at one side of the table, the guest at the other, and at the head and foot the master and mistress. Before Freya picked up her soup spoon, she crossed herself deliberately; the others paid her no notice. Bjorn Danielson addressed himself almost exclusively to Christy for the next half hour, and as the meal neared its end, he reached to a nearby chair and took a sheaf of papers covered with script and began to read the latest work he had completed. He planned to take it along to his lecture the next day. He was calling the long poem *The Death of Baldur* and this part dealt symbolically with Loki's punishment, his being chained with a serpent above that dropped venom on his face, while his wife tried to catch the poison in her cup. Whenever she bent to empty the cup the poison fell again on his face and Loki twisted in torment, causing the world of men to shake.

Clive said, when he had finished, "This is your greatest writing. It's genius!" He looked across at the daughters and wife, thinking suddenly that he had forgot genius was commonplace to them. How could they see this wonder that they lived with!

Lara laughed. "Let's have coffee in the other room."

They all got up, the old man rising as if reluctant, and following. Christy stood to one side, accepting a cup and then speaking hesitantly. "I ought to excuse myself. I have homework to go through."

"Excellent!" The poet beamed. "I see he's no sluggard."

"No ant either," Clive assured him.

Freya smiled from across the room. "Take along a piece of Lara's bakelser, won't you?"

"No, thank you. Good night all of you." He nodded and balancing his steaming cup went up the stairs, excitement spinning through his blood.

The time went by like wildfire. The golf clubs stood untouched, where Christy had set them the first day. He went through thirty rolls of film the first week. He photographed Bjorn Danielson with Loki and the granddaughter playing on the lawn. He asked Mrs. Danielson to bring her dishpan of peas out on the back porch and shell them there. She sat on the top step and he took a roll and a half in the brittle autumn sunlight. He remembered what her husband had said. "You write poetry too?"

She made a swift movement with her hand. "Nonsense. When I was very young, I thought I could write!"

"Was it hard to give up?"

"My pleasure has been to help Mr. Danielson."

"But of course."

"I haven't missed anything, Mr. Christy."

"Why don't you call me Clive as the girls do?"

She smiled, her eyes on her fingers. "I'll try." He snapped the shutter. That was the shot eventually published.

Christy sat down on the step below her. "I can't get used to the way you allowed me to walk into your family life."

"How long do you plan to stay, Clive?"

"He suggested March."

"Remember what it is exactly that you're here for, won't you?"

Christy thought it was an odd thing to say. "Of course."

She frowned, not looking at him. "Mr. Danielson's a strong-natured man."

"I've seen that."

"Freya was married for a while, you know."

"Yes."

"A writer. I thought it would go very well."

"I'm sorry. She seems happy."

"Life goes on, doesn't it?"

Lara came out on the porch above them. "Hallo. Are the peas done, Moder?"

Christy jumped up. "Stay a moment, Lara! Let me get one shot!"

"Nej, you silly." She laughed and took the peas and retreated to the kitchen.

He asked, "Has she a boyfriend?"

"She's always had admirers. Both my girls have. Don't you think it's a little windy out here?"

He watched her rise and walk in, her body tense. He was sorry, knowing that somehow inadvertently he'd hurt her.

In the nights he tried to sift through the reams of material that Bjorn Danielson kept heaping on his guest. In the free afternoons, the hour or two Danielson had first spent with Christy lengthened into three or four. He asked Christy to open his mail and started dictating replies, which Freya later typed. Freya also copied his manuscripts, sitting in the room beyond the two men, just past the open door, her back straight as a stick in her little chair, fingers beating rapidly on the keys. Lara and Mrs. Danielson sometimes were enlisted to make corrections. Nothing disturbed the three women's even composure. It began to seem to Clive that their eternal cheerfulness was forced.

One afternoon he went up to his room and, sitting on the cot, began to look over his notebook. He had no time to go through the film; that would have to come later when he returned to Washington. He was looking for some sort of design for the biography, something to give better direction to his jottings. There were steps outside the door and he got up to welcome the visitor before he could knock. Freya stood there, holding a dish of cookies.

"Moder and Lara just baked these and asked me to bring them to you. They say it's too early to spoil your supper."

"How nice." He took the plate. "And you. Please come in."

"Confusion confounded," she laughed, looking about.

"It is that. I'm getting nowhere fast, too. I'm trying to find a theme." He made way for the dish on the bureau, and pointed to the free space on the cot. "Will you sit?"

She ignored him. "Fader should be home from his lecture. He'll be needing you." Her voice took on an edge of mockery. "Better run. Hurry!" She went to the dormer window and looked through the tiny panes.

"I won't like leaving the view." He came to look at the December-rain-drenched campus over her shoulder.

She turned quickly, tipped her head a little to put her lips on his. He caught her about the neck and pressed her to him, trying to make the moment his. But she'd put her stamp on it, and he cursed himself because he'd let her make the move, not daring enough. He felt her withdraw and let his hands go.

Her eyes looked into his. She raised her brows, fingering her golden cross. "One thing might interest you, Clive." She smiled. "His name never was Bjorn Drang. That silly joke about a kyrka bell. It was always Danielson."

He didn't understand. "But why would he lie about such a thing?"

"I'm not an answer box."

He pulled her roughly to him. She didn't respond and when he released her, she stood looking down like Fröken Squiggle, underlip out. Then she stared at him with no hint of the usual placid smile. For the first time he noticed that she had her father's cruel mouth. "Why don't you get away from him, Freya? Why do you stay?"

"I was married for two years. My husband felt blessed when I couldn't bear him any more and went back to Fader."

"Will you never leave here?"

"And I have my church."

"You fool."

"How a fool, Confucius?"

"Loki."

"He speaks in riddles. A dog?" She laughed.

"A Norse demon. Oh Freya, you're being chained, poison's dripping onto your face. Don't you see?"

She leaned forward and kissed him again, this time matter-of-factly. He didn't move toward or away from it, neither repelled nor attracted. She walked to the door. "I probably shouldn't have brought you the sweets, Clive. Ja?" He heard her footfall go away. Later her voice rose below the window, "Where are you, Bruna? Time for milk!"

December passed. Christy didn't speak intimately with the younger daughter again. Freya made no opportunity. Danielson had given Lara and Christy a new task. They were to go through the cabinets of clippings that had stood in the hall. The duplicates were to be sifted out and the articles and new accounts pasted in a series of great black scrapbooks that Mrs. Danielson purchased. The task looked endless to Christy. And he was bothered by another letter he'd got from his publisher that morning asking for a definite report, threatening to withdraw support. He'd sent only postcards with photos of the St.

Jude Bell Tower and the new Archeology Building. "Wish you were here. All goes well." It didn't. Lara must have known what Christy was thinking. She applied some glue and looked across the desk at him.

"You never will, Clive."

"What?"

"Finish your book. Not as long as you're here."

"I like doing this. I want to."

"Don't be so belligerent."

"I get a feel of the material this way."

"The other one was like that for a long time, too."

Christy noticed Freya's typewriter had stopped pecking. "What other one?"

"You like golf, don't you?"

"Sure. What were you saying, Lara?"

"Let's make time and play a round. I think I can beat you."

"Good. At once. This afternoon."

She stopped him. "Tomorrow. When he has the lecture."

"My clubs have waited too long. Besides it's nice out there today. It may rain tomorrow."

"Nej."

"Are we Fröken Squiggles?" The typewriter began beating again. "Come on."

"I do want to." Lara's frown put years back onto her face. "Well, all right."

And so at three o'clock Christy shut the scrapbooks and backed his chair up. He went into the drawing room where Bjorn Danielson sat in a chair by the window, Loki curled at his feet. "Afternoon, sir."

The poet didn't look up and Christy felt the red of mortification begin behind his ears. "Lara and I are going around the golf course. We'll be back by five."

Danielson waited until he'd reached the door. "That's fine. You go along, you two. I'd come, but I've got to be an old gouty dodderer. Just be in the way."

"Not a bit of it," Christy said too quickly. "Wish you'd come."

"There's something else. I've been meaning to tell you to go ahead and pick out one of those canes of mine for yourself. You take any one you like. Go through the barrel. Don't hurry."

The guest hesitated. "That's very generous of you."

"Did you ever hear the story about the two pigeons and the cane? Now how does it go? The owner of the pigeons took them up on his roof to fly them. He turned them loose and they flew out in a great arc." Danielson paused. "I guess they— No— I forget it." He waved. "Well go along. Take your time choosing that stick."

Lara and Christy had a wonderful time. She kept shouting, "Breathe! Breathe!" the way her father did with the grandchild. He believed fresh air fed you like food. She had a better drive, but Christy sank his putts more accurately and so Lara beat him by only two points. She was jubilant as they got into the Fiat. "Let's not go home. Let's not, Clive!"

"All right. We'll eat out? I think I have enough money with me." He dug in his pocket.

"I have a little."

Christy phoned and spoke with Mrs. Danielson, saying they'd not be in for supper. "Have a nice evening, you two." She sounded pleased.

At a roadside dive they had beer and Brunswick stew and danced. By the time they got back into the car to head for the campus it was eleven-thirty. Christy was feeling great, and more or less casually put his arm on the back seat, leaned over and kissed Lara. "Had fun tonight?"

She didn't laugh back. "I love you."

"No. You're just feeling good, like me."

"But the other's true too. Not just tonight. I've been this way a long time. You don't have to be polite. I know you don't love me back. I wanted to say it once before you have to go."

"What do you mean go?"

"You'll be going."

He felt awkward, thinking, if it were her sister he'd be in a sizzle now. He took his arm back and started the car up. On the way home he asked what she'd meant in the afternoon when she said he was like the other one. "Who, Lara?"

"I love you, Clive." She laughed, gay. "I'll probably never say it again to anybody!"

The house was dark when they got home. Christy left their clubs in the car. It had got cold. Loki met them at the door, and they went at once to their rooms. The next morning went by as usual, Lara and Christy pasting up items, Freya taking Bruna to the nursery school and then settling to her typewriter. She nodded when she passed, her red-blond hair shining; Christy could feel Lara's eyes watching his follow Freya.

In the afternoon Bjorn Danielson astounded his guest by coolly stating, as he put down the last piece of correspondence, "I think your work is finished here, Mr. Christy."

"It's scarcely begun!"

"You've been here since early October. Three months is a lot of time to give to a biographer."

"I've spent all of it working for you."

"And you've been paid ten times over. You've seen greatness at work."

Christy thought he might be joking. "Mr. Danielson, you mean that?"

He rose, his cold eyes on Christy. Freya's eyes, Christy thought. "Stupid fellow. I'm throwing you out. Don't know what I was thinking of, bringing you here into a houseful of women."

"You do well enough in it."

"You are a sneak of the first order. Ja, a sneak. I shall see whether something's missing from the papers I so thoughtlessly put in your hands."

It was beginning to sound familiar to Christy. "Who was Freya's husband? Tell me! Tell me, sir. Was it the one who wrote *The Chain of Gleipner?* I'm sure of it." Christy left Danielson and ran to the door.

The voice followed. "Get out of here at once!"

He passed Mrs. Danielson as he ran up the stairs. She appeared terrified, a wrinkled old hag, skin yellow. *God dag, Astrid!* Of the "blue-black, river-black hair."

He knew Freya's room. She wasn't in it. He dashed to the nursery. She had pulled the shades and Bruna's eyes were closed. Freya turned as he came in and lifted a warning hand. "Hush, Clive! What is it?"

He grasped her arm, his whisper hoarse. "Who was your husband? Did he live in your home for a few weeks like me? Did you bring cookies to his room? Did he write that whining groveling book about that beast?"

She stared at him, impassive. "Let me go."

"Answer."

"Certainly, it was he. This is our child."

Christy pulled her to him. He felt she was being tormented, and he tried to sense whether she loved him at all. He held his hands gently on her slim shoulders and forced himself to tenderness. She responded like a wooden doll. He took his lips from hers. "Freya!"

"I asked you to let me go." She had taken the cross in her fingers.

"All right. But it's like a mirror, clear all of a sudden. Listen, I'm leaving, but I want you to marry me. I'll write you what to do."

She was smiling. "Foolish Clive. The hero rescues the maid from the fire-breathing dragon! Go home. I prefer it here."

Christy dropped his arm and wheeled and left the room. He threw his things together as quickly as he'd done in the fall when he left Washington. He took his package of notes, leaving the poet's papers in disordered heaps on the floor of his room. There was one more thing to do. Lara was waiting on the back porch steps when he went out the door, as he'd hoped. He stood looking down at her. "Goodbye, Lara."

"It's just as well. Whether it's sooner or later, it has to be." She was pale, her freckles standing out; her hands clasped each other. "Good luck." She put one hand out.

He set down the bags and took it. "Lara. Do you want to come with me? I'll marry you."

She shook her head. "Thanks for asking."

He picked up the grips and walked away from the house. He drove over the winding blacktop campus road and onto the four-lane highway. He was going through the Baltimore Tunnel before he'd decided not to scrap the book entirely. When he reached Washington, he felt even enthusiastic.

He holed up in his efficiency and in four months had a completed manuscript. Christy felt it wrote itself. He hoped it wasn't too noticeably a chant of praise. He'd tried to hold down the homage, the hero worship, that charged through it. He wanted to title it *The Frost Giant.* In the old legend, the giant was formed out of vapor, and from his body had come the earth, the oceans, the trees, the heavens; from his eyebrows the fence that marked off earth, the home of man. Christy thought the title suited the book's framework. His publisher and sales manager agreed. They took the plane down to see him and look over the finished work. He could tell they were more than pleased. Late in the afternoon they went over to a bar on Connecticut to celebrate. It was a spring evening, and Christy tapped his walking stick as they strolled along. It had the open-fanged Norse serpent carved in the black wood, over Loki's face.

"Skål!" Christy had begun to feel very good.

"A sure bet, this one is!" His publisher slapped the counter top with two fingers. "We figure on a best seller."

"You should see the advance orders, Mr. Christy!" The sales manager swayed. "Have another."

"Thanks." He was on his third. "That reminds me of a

The Other One

story. Ever hear this one? There was a dog thought he was a rooster. So one day he walked into a henhouse. He looked around and— Well, let me see. I think there was a hen and— No—" He paused while they waited for the rest. "I forget how it goes." Christy waved a hand airily. "It was funny though." He laughed to himself. "Ja."

"Here, have another," his publisher urged.

Matthew

Matthew reached the fence as usual at almost half past seven that evening, standing overalled, sandy-haired, his back muscle-humped, six foot four in his work shoes. Rachel was in the rocker outside their doorstep, the last of the sun gathered in her apron where a bit of sewing lay forgot. Her face wore an indrawn look. Her black hair had loosed from its band and the shorter ends curled about her ears, sharply defined against her white skin. Behind her was the clapboard house they'd been renting a year and a half, its two small rooms adequate. They liked it out in Stringtown, though it made a long walk for Matthew to and from the mill village each day. Rachel had a sister who lived there in one of the box-like houses the Company constructed when it built the knit-goods factory, staking off dirt streets and plots, laying boards for sidewalks. This house had no conveniences like those. Put together with spit and string, it was tired out from many tenants. Matthew had done a good job of repairing it on Sundays. Rachel had bought crash at eleven cents a yard and made curtains and a cloth to spread on the table. Matthew got a piece of rug from the commissary at Christmas that was high but he felt worth the price. Last month in April when he whitewashed, he gave the shed and outhouse a coat too. The garden where corn and okra were spiring stood in a pattern of unfolding green on brown, for Rachel kept it well hoed. The only fault here had been the lack of trees. Last fall when the sap went down they dug young dogwood and elm in the woods behind their lot, and for four bits Matthew got from a peddler two sapling London poplars. The landlord gave them leave to set them out. All had caught and greened; they stood about the yard like spindly step-children not sure of a welcome.

Rachel heard the gate latch and her look changed. "Matt! I figured you'd never come." She sprang down the path like a girl though her life was half over.

Her skin was sun-warm. The man looking down at her thought how the one thing she wanted that would seem easiest to give, he seemed unable to give her. "Say, one of the power looms broke down today. The boss is that riled. The treadles won't budge. I says, Mr. Slatterley, the main shaft's cracked."

"You can fix it. You're the best shop overseer he ever took on."

"You know how these new machines are. Too much to them I claim. Give me one of those looms like we had in the overall mill where first I went to work, the parts fair out in the open so you can see what's going on. That was before these new fangled safety laws come in."

"Sure to God you're the strongest fellow in the mill."

"We had the housing off by quitting time. I says to the boss, we'll have it in shape sometime tomorrow."

"You're sharp, Matt."

"Maybe with a machine." He bent to pull a weed from beside the path.

"Did you see Jim Ed?"

"I pretty near forgot, Rachel. Your sister's gone to the hospital."

"She wasn't due till Sunday week! You should have told me. Millie's time!"

"The office got the phone call late in the morning. The boss gave Jim Ed off to take her in. Reckon it's come by now?"

"Wish I knew." They had come into the house and Rachel went to the ice safe to take out the fatback. There were a few pictures tacked on the walls, mostly from old calendars, and a likeness of Shirley Temple: "Curlylocks." Above the stove was a faded photo of a child of three in white dress and bonnet. Rachel had picked flowers from the woods and set them in a crock on the treadle Singer machine in one corner. She was turning the fat meat in the black iron pan she set on the kerosene stove. "When I had her there," she said and motioned up to the likeness, "I was told never one come easier to this world."

Rachel looked over to her husband, who was washing at the sink. He had poured water from the kettle into an enameled pan and was scrubbing the brush on the yellow soap bar and rubbing at his arms so the suds foamed. "Can scarcely get this monkey-grease off!"

"You mind me talking about her, Matt?"

"Say, you ever dwell on him?"

"My first husband? No. But once in a while I dream about that day, the knocking when it came near supper time. I was making pies up. Since then I just can't care for blueberries. Those men talking to me about the crash, saying I was to go with them. We'd let the insurance lapse so the factory wouldn't give me a thing." She lifted the crisp pork onto a plate and began slicing potatoes swiftly into the crackling fat, the scent lifting and spreading. "Mostly, Matt, I can't disremember that baby there."

"Wouldn't be right if you did."

She looked over and laughed sharply. "When I'm alone, now and then I talk to that picture and make out as if she's here."

"Don't get worked up, now." Matthew got up to take the bucket from the sideboard. "I'll fetch some new water. I'd as soon drink it cold at the table." When he was out in back he knelt to clean away the weeds about the wood well cover.

Matthew

"Maybe she'd take to a pup or a kitten. She'll want a child the worst fashion now her sister's got hers."

He drew his hand back swift. A snake was winding in a sluggish way out from the old boards lining the well-top, a timber rattler. Matthew ran for a stick and struck it. He took it by its tail, slinging it at the ground to crush its head, throwing it off toward a ditch. He saw the reason for its slowness. By the boards squirmed a nest of a dozen miniature rattlers, just born. He crushed them with stick and heel, gathered them and the handful of weeds he'd let fall, and threw them all on the compost heap he was saving to put on the garden. He went back in.

Rachel was folding away the cloth of blue and white cotton, which matched her curtains. She'd sewn them in winter using a close stitch. She starched them a little so the material seemed of fine quality. She moved firm-stepped, setting out on the bare wood table, scrubbed to the color of milk, the dimestore cutlery and gray-white stoneware and a bowl of lettuce and white radishes. She put out the glass jar of cider vinegar that Matthew liked on his greens.

Matthew spoke up. "How would you like a dog for yourself, Rachel? One of the new hands has a brute that's whelped and he's seeking homes for them."

"I expect I'd like one."

"It would be company. And a guard too, not that there's anything to fear." He pulled his chair out. "I'll speak for one then. Come now and sit."

"I want to get the bread."

"I'll get it."

"No. I want to do for you."

"You baby me." He bit his lip on the word.

She never noticed. "You work too hard. Let me go to the mill with you, Matt. We wouldn't have to be skimping so careful. I used to work in a cutting room and my eyes are still as good as when I was young. Why I enjoyed it!"

"I'd as leave my wife didn't work. So long as we can make out."

"Millie stayed at the knitter till she was eight months along."

"And she looked peaked too. You know who sent her home? It wasn't her man, Jim Ed. It was Slatterley, afraid she was fixing to drop it there."

"They were strapped for money."

"That's no reason."

"It would keep me busy, Matt." She brought the loaf and sat. "I'm thinking of Millie and where she is right now."

In the night Matthew slept without stirring. A sprinkle of rain started up and mounted to a downrushing. The saplings in the yard lifted their leaves and the dogwoods held up their petals so the dust that had drifted from the road ran off. The flow abated and as dawn came on birds began to warble and cry. Rachel lay listening to them and the dripping from the gutters on each side of the house. Matthew had tarred the leaks and the rain was guided into two barrels. It was the best water for washing clothes; it made hair silken too. There had been no barrels at the place where she started housekeeping as a young woman years ago. But she had taken pans into the yard to collect it and always washed the baby girl's hair in the soft water.

Footsteps came thudding on the road in the distance. Closer and louder. Closer! Then a fist on the door. "Matt?" She shook his shoulder.

He pushed at the covers and swung his legs out, drawing on the pair of overalls on the rug, slipping up the straps, stumbling into the kitchen. "Cut out that racket! I'm on my way."

"Open up. This here's Jim Ed!"

Matthew turned the key. The stocky form of Rachel's brother-in-law plunged in and stood head down like a bull. The silence was heavy. Matthew shook the man's shoulder. "Is it Millie? What's the cause with you?"

The figure was swaying in the dawnlight, the odor of whisky swinging faint from it. "Dead." Jim Ed hiccuped. "Millie is. She's gone for sure."

Rachel came in the doorway. Her white gown flooded about her shape. "Millie?"

"She's dead and she ain't ever coming back. Now listen here. I'm quitting Mill Village." The man made a gesture as if dragging aside a curtain, his voice sullen. "If I stayed it might just come on me to kill someone, starting with that hammerhead calls himself the Company doctor. And maybe next old Boss Slatterley who makes his slaveys jump. Am I drunk, Matt?" Jim Ed had begun to giggle. Then his voice broke, "And I'd slay the youngun to boot."

Rachel breathed, "It's alive?" She hadn't moved.

"I give it to you, Rachel. I seen you looking at Millie lots of times. Like one robbed of her own whelps. You can have it."

"No," Matthew said. "I won't have it. Besides, you might beg it back from her later."

"Not me, Matt. For all your bull-back and knowing ways, they say you're but a steer. Here's your chance to satisfy Rachel." The man drew his hand trembling over his face. His mouth shook. "I'm undone. Sorry I said that. I'm fair undone."

"You clear out of here." Matthew moved forward uneasy, hunching his bare shoulders and back. "Before I knock you down."

"Wait." The woman was motionless, her eyes brilliant. "I'd as soon take Millie's baby."

"I won't give in." Matthew gritted his teeth.

"Settle it between you as you please." Jim Ed shrugged. "Makes me no nevermind. I'm not staying even to bury Millie. There's no insurance so you let the county have her. But don't allow them to lay her in a plain box painted prime red, the way they took and buried one of my sisters. You watch out for that, Rachel, and stand up for a decent coffin."

"I will, Jim Ed."

"And I'm not drawing my last blue slip neither. Let Slatterley buy him some lightning on my pay to remember me by. I'm riding the next northbound train. I aim to take up where I left off at when I married Millie."

"Is it a boy or girl?" Rachel whispered.

"Hold your tongue," Matthew cried. "You see he's off his head."

"I never asked or cared." Jim Ed looked at Rachel. "But it's what killed my wife. And I make you a present of it." He turned into the singing birds and the ashy sky and shuffled away.

"It's the hand of providence, Matt."

"I don't favor much the way you're taking this."

"We have a child!"

"We don't."

"It's my sister's. My own blood."

"Not mine."

"Take me to the hospital."

His voice was uncolored. "Don't you see I can't?"

"Matt?" She put her hand on his arm.

"Think on me. My pride!"

"Let your pride go for this. I know what I'm asking. And it's easier to lift a mountain on the point of a needle than to root pride up from a man's heart. Matt?"

"They'll snigger." His hands hung clenched. "In the stockroom. When my back's turned aways."

"Let them. What does it mean, if we have a child? If we must and there's not a thing else to do."

He sighed. "Then let you have your way."

While he sat on the bed edge lacing his rough-leather shoes, she undid her hair, combing it and fastening it back. She took her light coat and he the cap he wore on Sundays. They followed Jim Ed's tracks to the wet highway bordered with a few houses and named Stringtown. They walked single-file when the going was bad, Matthew ahead.

When the ground was even, Rachel joined him. "We never said goodbye to Jim Ed. Reckon we'll lay eyes on him again?"

"He'd not have taken notice."

"Or thanked him either. Everything ended in one night for Jim Ed. Wife, baby, job. The way it was with me that time, Matt. Till you came."

"I'm not much."

"You're sharp, Matt."

"I haven't made out by you as I've wanted."

"Mr. Slatterley and me, we couldn't either of us get on without you!"

They separated as the road narrowed and when she caught up again she asked, "Think Jim Ed'll be coming back some day?"

"Studying on that still?"

"I doubt it. Millie wasn't uncommon contented here." In a while she said, "Matt, I heard Jim Ed call you a slavey. Do you feel that about the mill?"

"Some do. Me, I favor the shop. My people worked always in mills. My daddy started when he was nine and they'd consent to take him on. At ten cents a day. You couldn't hold him at home. I care for work for its own sake. They say man is born to work as the bird to flying. There's men coming around raising sand about hardships. Talking about organizing. But I'm not so sure. I labor not for that blue slip. And I was going to tell you after a while. Mr. Slatterley says to me that Jim Ed's been slacking the everlasting time and he was about to lay him off."

"Then I reckon it's better him quitting on his own."

The sunrise had flamed about the sky and as the colors faded and the day settled into morning, the couple were walking on the plank sidewalk alongside the deserted main street and going up the steps of the frame building called the Company Hospital.

It was a boy. No one questioned their right to him, Rachel being his aunt. It seemed to her, when she picked him up in his unbleached flannel coverlet, as if the garden were hoed, the gutters patched, and all made ready for his coming.

Matthew felt differently. From the first he stood away. It was she carried the bundle the few blocks from the hospital to the commissary. She took from her pocket the doctor's list of what had to be purchased before Matthew could go to the mill that day. She waited on the porch until he strode out with the paper sack on his arm. "Had to sign a chit for it, Rachel. Against my pay. Don't let it slip my mind."

"I won't."

They walked back down the highway. Matthew had the eleven to seven shift so there was time enough for him to see them home before he left. Rachel put the baby on a pillow in the wash basket. She set it on the iron-legged storage box in the bedroom and shut the door. "I'll have your breakfast in a flash, Matt!" She was lighting the oven and taking the flour from the shelf.

That night when he came to the gate, the infant was in a quilt in Rachel's apron where she rocked outside the door. "Do you mind that I've called him Marvel?" she called.

"That's a bookish name!" he hurried by to wash the grease from his arms and face.

"I made it up."

"If it is a name," he added.

She followed him in. "Look, while I put the supper on, will you hold him?"

"Rachel, don't manage me with honied ways." He looked down at the two from his crooked height. "I'm fair worn out. Had to tear that whole god-forsaken loom down. Didn't get it back either. Mr. Slatterley's in a sweat. He's laid some of the weaving girls off till Tuesday week."

She put the baby in the basket. "I'll learn him to say Daddy first thing."

Matthew

"You'll not. Nor uncle neither." He ran the comb through his sand-colored hair. "And have you still got a notion for that cur pup?"

"I expect Marvel'll want to play with one in time."

"I wasn't thinking of play, but rather that I've seen a snake or two about." Matthew spoke quietly.

"Take one then. And say why he shouldn't call you Daddy when you're raising him and paying his feed."

"I took notice what was passing in that hand's mind when he asked about the pup. Thinks he, the gelding's got him a foal. That's what they say." He put a hand out and flushed. "Truth is the water of life. Let the truth stand, Rachel."

"I've no right to feel as good as I do, Matt. There's Millie being laid under sod on Sunday and Jim Ed run off nobody knows where." She went to bring the hot pans to the table. "That store milk sets good with him. He'll be a sizeable man!"

Matthew refused to look and sat down to gaze at his food and stir it absently, mixing the green pickle relish into the steaming kidney beans colored like dried locusts.

Marvel's mother was buried by the county in a yellow pine box for which Matthew had to go in debt. Afterward, later in the day, some of the mill people felt obliged to say a few words about the dead. Matthew went by to listen so he could report to Rachel. The church sexton, an old man, had built a pulpit in his back yard and strung some fifteen-watt bulbs over it. Anyone who could pull a few listeners could preach there summer evenings.

"As all you know," one of the women pattern cutters shouted, "Millie never ran around. All of us are going to miss her two hands at that knitting machine."

"Hear, hear!" There was some clapping. "Amen!"

"Next year," a pale young janitor called out, "she'd have been a full fashion knitter!"

"Amen! Shout glory!" And that was taken up by everybody.

Then a new woman learner rose to say that it hadn't been

true of Millie that when poverty came in the door, love went out the window. She had cared for her husband and he'd taken and run off broken-hearted, leaving the youngun to her sister to rear. At this point Matthew walked away from the group.

Marvel did well under his aunt's care. When a traveling camera man came to the door one day she gave him thirty-five cents to take a picture of the child in her lap and the yellow dog at her feet. It came in the mail three weeks later. It was a good impression and she tacked it up beside the faded photo of the small girl over the stove.

Never at any time would Matthew hold the boy on his lap or play with him. He tried. At Christmas he brought home a knobby paper-mesh stocking from the commissary. It was crammed with tin toys that rusted quickly and had to be thrown out. He fashioned a crib that swung up out of the way to save space in the bedroom. He began to buy fewer clothes for himself, allowing his shirts and overalls to get a bit more ragged and whitened than formerly so there would be coins in the stone bowl for Rachel to buy what was needed. Before others, Matthew made a point of calling Marvel "Jim Ed's boy."

The child was two the spring a letter arrived from Jim Ed, reporting how he'd joined up with the navy and was putting out to other lands. He didn't mention the boy, but said he was remarried and was taking this occasion to thank Rachel and Matthew for seeing to the proper burying of his first wife. He had been working in a chair factory in New York state and allowed he had had a gut full.

One evening in July Rachel was waiting for Matthew's return, unpinning clothes from the line, keeping one eye on Marvel in the dooryard grasping at shadows. The mill had already blown the next shift. Clover dried on stems and the perfume was heavy upon the sunshine. The dog was sleeping on the threshold near Marvel. The boy was plump, tow-haired, and had learned to walk in a swift kind of totter.

When Rachel looked back the cur slept alone. She ran to find the little boy in the back yard by the well. He wrinkled his face and held his breath, trying to decide if he should cry or not. He held his arm to her and she saw the two bright fang marks, and in another glance the old viper sliding off among the leaves, having dropped a few young under the boards. She fell to her knees and began to suck at the marks, spitting. The child began to wail, sensing her anguish.

The front gate slapped, and Matthew came running up. "Curse the dog for worthless!"

"Matt! Save him!"

"I will," he gasped, unfolding the blade of his knife and cutting over the pinpoints while he held the soft arm. When it bled, he pulled out his red kerchief and bound it above the wound. He plucked the child from the grass and ran out the gate. Down the road he trotted, away from Rachel, until the dirt became blacktop. Swinging on toward the town, his breath heavy.

A long black car with a California plate in front stopped beside him, the dust swirling. "How about a lift?" The fat man was shirt-sleeved, his coat crumpled on the back seat.

"Jim Ed's boy's snake-bit!"

"My gosh! Get in, my friend. You're a mill hand, aren't you? Where'll I drive you?"

Matthew pointed. "Thataway!"

Marvel had ceased sobbing; he laid his head against the rough bib of Matthew's overalls. The large hand was holding his. He breathed a long sigh and pulled in his lower lip.

"Wait till I tell the missus about this," the city man cried.

"You can bear to the left at the fork there." Matthew wondered if Rachel was trailing down the road on foot. He had lost all sense of time. He spoke through his teeth. "You can stop ahead where that old stake says hospital."

"Anything else I can do? How's the little guy doing?"

"Thanks, Cap." Matthew forgot to close the car door when he got out with Marvel. He ran up the steps.

The doctor left his other patients when he heard and hurried in. While he gave the serum injection the boy didn't cry but fixed his eyes on Matthew's face. "I'll send a nurse in," the doctor said, "to tell you where he's to sleep. I want him here for twenty-four hours. Your son's got as much grit as I've ever seen!"

Matthew tried out the word when they were alone. "Easy, son." He regretted his bad manners in not shutting that car door as they'd got out. Matthew liked to be particular about such things.

By the time Rachel arrived, the two had washed up and Marvel was sleeping on a cot behind a screen. He had Matthew's thumb in his fist and the man sat on the cot next to his, leaning over so the child could keep his hold.

"How's he faring?" Rachel's voice was there, like a stranger's. He saw her dusty shoes and felt her fear. "Nurse said you were so quick getting him here!"

"I was blessed to get a lift."

"Matt, a boy belongs to the one who cares for him."

"The doctor allowed he was mine. Your son's gritty, he says to me."

"Matt, you can't oppose it any more."

"It's been a plague to me, Rachel, that I couldn't give you one."

"Did I complain? I knew what I had in you."

"You wanted one the worst."

"And I got one."

He felt the might in him then surging in his bones, in his rounded back that had more strength in it than any man's at the mill. He sensed how his power flowed into the child, how it would live because he'd given it life. He stayed there by the blue ward light until the three o'clock shift whistled into the night outside. He drew his hand away. Rachel pulled up the dark blanket, and he went back down the road.

When he reached their yard the yellow beast hurled itself in yelps to greet him. He drew his foot back to kick it but let it go. "Not your fault, I guess. Could anything be done twice it'd be done better. But you got to learn to catch snakes."

He stumbled over Rachel's basket of clothes that she'd abandoned. He pulled off his overalls and big shoes. Wakeful, he sat by the window, his big-knuckled thumb against his cheek. In the soft wind outside in the garden, growing things were ripening. The two poplars rose like dark pillars, and the elm trees spouted in the fogging moonlight like funnels of blue smoke.

What's Mine Is Yours

"But clearly I remember it, wife. Eh? How could you forget?" Pierre's face had lost its firmness over the years, but his big body remained supple, for he took care of it, going to the gym after he left his office daily. And his manner was still winning, Yvonne thought, when he made a special effort, when there were people about. The party was over and the pair slumped back in their chairs, too weary to go at once to bed. Pierre removed his coat and leaned forward, forgetting his pipe, so the ashes spilled on the living room rug. He kicked at them with his shoe toe, grinding them in.

Yvonne tapped a cigarette and put it in her holder, her eyes glancing over at him. "I've been honest with you from the start, *chéri*." She was rather fox-like with her red bushy hair, her eyes, which were her most prominent feature, moist and dark. She moved to adjust the orange sweater she had thrown on. "If I'd gone sneaking in some letters of yours once, why you know I'd have been the first to say so."

"I found them stuffed back. Naturally, a thing like that, I recall very well."

"Why didn't you bring it up at the time?"

"I refused to believe it, to think such a thing of my wife. Eh?" He spilled more pipedust and rubbed his shoe on it again. "It was shocking, I can tell you."

"Nonsense."

"No." He thrust his pipe in his mouth and tore a match from a folder. He struck it. "It is not so."

Her eyes followed his movements, thinking: he does it as if it were his first attempt with tobacco. "I noticed Helen Todd having quite a time with you tonight. Better watch her."

"You changing the subject? Eh?" Pierre flushed and laid his pipe down with a harsh sound in the tray.

"Don't you want to talk about Helen Todd?"

"All right. What is it I did wrong?"

"She wanted you to dance, and you rushed into the kitchen. I saw her follow. What was going on in there?"

"And you saw me come right out with the sandwiches, Mrs. Detective. And Helen with the coffee."

"Remember well, don't you? Why are you on the defensive, *chéri?*" She was like a vixen yapping. "Don't hide things."

"Who's hiding?" Pierre bellowed, at bay.

"There you go! Were you in the kitchen to prove something, perhaps?" Yvonne's hands lay still, palms up in her lap as if she were quite unmoved.

"Always it comes to where I'm denying something, wife. You never take my word, do you?"

"The point is, you've no confidence in yourself. You know how you are." She crushed her cigarette and sighed. "Don't I remember when I was young, how you'd say, we're one. What's yours is mine, what's mine is yours."

His pipe burned deserted in the tray. His fingers turned to the soft cloth of the chair arm, digging into it so they almost tore it. Pierre raised his head, like a poised animal. "And what about those letters?"

She selected another cigarette from the ebony box. She brushed at the tobacco shreds in the orange wool. She seemed to be leashing herself. "The letters. Humm."

"Naturally, I couldn't think you'd pried into something that was mine." His eyes hunted about her face as she scratched the match and puffed the smoke in a cloud.

Yvonne smiled to herself, puckering her lips in a little pout. "You've made up the incident. Is that it? You don't have proof!"

"How do you mean?"

"Why, the letters. Produce these marvels."

"No. I don't have them, it's true."

"*Petite chou,* if I cared to comb this house, do you know I wouldn't be surprised to come across them? Could you have intentionally forgot where you put them?"

"Hardly." He stood up from the chair, his body awkward the way a large animal's sometimes is. Leaning over the table, tapping the pipe so the ashes fell into the metal dish. Fumbling for his coat, putting it on.

"Now run away, *chéri,*" Yvonne began to bark, "as you always do. We never talk our way through anything. If you've no confidence or respect for yourself, you see why others have none for you. Why Helen Todd thought it was okay to trail you into the kitchen!" Her voice broke on a high key. Her eyes flinched when the door banged. She heard him take his stick from the closet. He would go for a walk as he often did. She ought to follow. She toyed with it. There was a chance he met someone out there. Helen Todd?

As a matter of fact, Yvonne did remember his letters. She refused to discuss it only because it was so senseless. They'd been married almost a year when they'd had their first silly quarrel. She couldn't remember now what it was about, perhaps he'd neglected to kiss her when he went out in the morning. At any rate she'd become upset, weeping all the day, raging at Pierre when he returned in the evening, after his exercise at the gym. He'd been astonished, apologizing for his morning rudeness. Somehow after that incident, a change was evident in him. He seemed to drift, unattentive. Yvonne had pricked up her ears at it. He'd be in his den with a stack of papers he was preparing for his firm. She'd go in to kiss him and he'd be stiff and formal. *Cherchez la girlfriend,* she told herself eagerly. She began to come home unexpectedly now and then, but Pierre was alone always. He might get up and walk to where Yvonne was in the doorway, his kiss grudging. One day she caught him closing and locking the bottom drawer to his desk.

Yvonne spent a lot of time searching for the key, digging through his possessions, replacing them carefully. When she came on a green-tinted envelope with his name in green ink on the face, she was elated, but it was only a bill forwarded by one of the office girls. She ferreted in the bookshelves and behind the picture frames. She discovered it on a rainy morning tucked just under the blotter flap. Quickly she unlocked the drawer to run to earth what she sought. It was concealed far under everything else, a sheaf of envelopes bound with a worn string. Yvonne grasped them, running to the gray window light, seeking the name. But it was nothing after all, so she had to shake her head at herself. She continued leafing through them, until she thought she heard the front door close. She put them back and locked the latch. She went, a little disappointed perhaps, to greet him.

Pierre had nodded as she came from his den. His umbrella dripped a moment on the floor before he turned away and went down the hall to put it in the stand to dry. Convinced for the time of his fidelity, Yvonne promised herself and had made it her duty thereafter to tell Pierre every night that she cared for him. No matter how she felt. What's mine is yours, *petit chou*, she'd say, and what's yours is mine. Forever, you know? One time idly, a few months later, she went to look at the letters, but they weren't under the papers in the drawer as before.

Pierre strode back on the pavement now, returning from his walk. It was autumn and the nights were invested with the sweetened odor of drying dropping leaves. The odor of death. The falling hairs of old autumn. What is it they say? *Gray hairs and autumn leaves are death's blossoms.* Moonlight was washing over everything, making it blue and strange. Pierre went up

Children and Lovers

the front steps, clacking his cane vigorously. He closed the door and stepped into the living room. "Sorry I made a scene, wife. Eh? That's all I wanted to say."

"It's all right." She brushed her bright hair back with a stoic hand.

"Go to bed now."

"Don't you want to come up too, *chéri?*" The smile pursed her lips.

"No. First I'll smoke a pipeful."

She fingered the orange buttons on her sweater. "If you prefer."

"Good night."

Pierre turned abruptly and went down the carpeted hall to the den. He shut the door after him softly. In the dusky light, he set his stick in the corner and drew off his black coat. He thrust it aside as if it were the peel of his daily living. He sat down on the side of the hard couch, leaning his elbows on his knees. In the window the moon made a square of bluish light. Pierre's eyes were shiny, unmasked in his dark face. He was listening to his wife groping up the stairs to the bedroom. Yvonne would take off her clothes and hang them carefully on hooks. She would cream her face with little up-strokes like a marmoset. She would brush her hair that was like a tree on fire and don her nightdress and lie unsleeping until Pierre would come.

Yvonne had dug into his letters that time. She'd jammed them back when he came home. How often had she stood shuffling them, peering? Clearly she could not have forgot! It was Yvonne's way to say she had. She'd swear she saw a cat sitting on an empty staircase if she wanted. And that the sky was made of blue silk. What succor Pierre had taken from that scrawling child's script! Ah, it was true, he had been trying to escape into another time. It was idle-minded of him. He was weak; no doubt of it. Which was why people took advantage of him, as Yvonne said. She was right about Helen Todd too.

Pierre had had to push Helen off hard and grab the tray and get out. People read something into Pierre that he didn't know himself was there. All he knew was that he had a great desire to be well regarded. Eh?

The letters had been a kind of secret, though there had been no reason to withhold them from his wife. Long ago, after some misunderstanding with Yvonne, he'd almost wept one night, upon awakening from a dream of his dead brother. The night had been much like this one, things a little unclear because of the blue colored light that came from the ghastly orb that ruled above. Recollections had swarmed in his brain. Pierre had been parent as well as loving companion to his brother. At the time of Armand's funeral he thought he'd not have the courage to look ever again at anything that had belonged to the youth. But when his wife went out one day, so he had the house alone, Pierre climbed thoughtfully to the attic and probed about in the junk there. In a trunk they'd used to take along when their aunt sent them to summer camp, under musty breeches and coats and long brown leather boots, he uncovered them. He'd carried them down to his den.

Armand came alive and the old boyhood days! The free everlasting summertime! The two were close. A thought born in one's mind would be declared by the other the next moment. Armand died when Pierre was twenty-two. The black horse reared up and killed the impetuous boy who'd never been afraid, who loved the big colts that belonged to their aunt, even when they laid their ears along their skulls and bared their stained teeth. Armand gave them apples, and they rubbed their noses against his forearm and curved their long necks. The boy had insisted on taking the tricky black out that hot day when horseflies were hugging sluggish to beasts' shivering skins, stinging like whips. Stiff-backed, Armand had cantered off. After it happened, Pierre avoided his aunt's stables. And when he went with Yvonne to the inn on their honeymoon, he refused curtly to ride. They'd almost had a dispute about it. His love hadn't been enough to overcome his feeling. It was the beginning of his failures to his wife.

The letters became a small relief in Pierre's days. They held reality in re-creation. He formed a habit of taking them out when dispirited. He would lean back in his swivel chair and his jagged spirit would be ironed smooth. In the room's pale light, he retreated into the far past. Armand shouted while the sun glazed his brown figure. He raced wild over the greensward ahead of Pierre, laughing. Whatever they did, they did together. They never felt orphans! They wrote each other when apart, crude silly notes about nothing. Pierre wondered why he had ever preserved the nonsense. But leafing through them, forgetting time, he was grateful.

When his wife came in from shopping or tea or her appointments, he returned them quickly to the drawer and turned the key. His breath came fast, almost as if he felt guilt for an illicit thing, as if it were a harm to Yvonne. Then once he walked home early from the office, not stopping for his usual gym workout. It was drizzling and as Pierre entered the door, he heard her moving in his den. As she came out, he knew. As he turned away to put his umbrella to drip, quite truly he knew. He held his tongue, but at his first chance, Pierre went to examine the crooked knot, the slight disarray. The next time she was away, he destroyed them, burning every one in the fireplace. When the ashes were cold, he scooped them into a pan and threw them in the garbage. He opened the windows even, so there should be no scent or sign. It was as if his brother, Armand, had died twice.

Now Pierre could hear the small noises upstairs in the bedroom. He rose and went from the room, down the halls, locking the front and back doors. Subdued in movement, he almost could articulate how he felt caged by this little woman. At the bottom of the stairs, he looked up. The lost days of boyhood where his brother ran were becoming a dim dream.

Pierre put a foot on the first step and pinched his trouser-leg, frowning. Why had he not demanded an explanation years ago when he found his wife had unlocked his desk? Eh? He'd behaved almost as though he were in the wrong. And a few minutes ago they'd quarreled about it again as if it would do any good. It was no use with Yvonne. She said what she pleased, called the sun the moon, said red was green. And that she cared for him! What's yours is mine, *petit chou*, and what's mine is yours! Pierre chuckled. Well, despite it all, it was Yvonne had set him free. It was all right. After the accident, Pierre had been at wit's end, simply lost. Then who had stepped forward to save him, marrying him, Yvonne! That was the debt. Pierre went up the stairs. Armand had been wrong about Yvonne; she made a splendid wife. And isn't it said: *There is no sweet without sour?*

He sniffed the burning tobacco. "You're smoking in bed. Eh?"

"No, of course not. Why do you ask, *chéri?*"

Pierre shook his head to himself, smiling. "I just want to keep you safe. Naturally, I care about you, you know!" Pierre quickened his steps, almost gay.

My Old Lady

I never wanted to go to St. George Polytechnic Institute in the first place, but Dad was all for it. He's Old Corps. That was the way with half of us there. The Corps'll make a man of you, son. Yeah. Grow you six foot six. Turn you into an A. Lincoln. Balls it will! Take me now. I'm pretty average, sort of untidy. That used to bother my mother. She was happy though with my school record. Even as a kid I was what they call here a Jewel, my grades a little too high. Why, I might even get the scholastic ribbon.

The wind was pushing over the flat Indiana campus and through our barracks-hole window. I got up and looked out; the sun wasn't due up for another hour, one of those dusky mornings when the Indian summer air smelled of running water and mountain fields. Made me think of Deer Hill back home on Mr. Bledsoe's place. I wondered if the blacktails had come down from the high timber yet.

The band-orderly's bugle yelped outside, and it was 6:05. The snore of Mike, my old lady, which is what you call your roommate, stopped. He hauled himself from bed and over to the sink where he splashed cold water around like a spaniel. We began to dress. This afternoon they'll march us over to the Athletic Field, where we'll wave our caps on order and cheer ourselves silly for the good old Corps. Then we'll use our passes to go home for Thanksgiving. Six whole days off Tech! The first part of tonight I'll spend packed in Pablo Soliel's car. He'll drop me in Ordinary Bend, Oklahoma, on his way to Albuquerque. I've already given him my IOU for five berries but to him it's just a token. He's got a yellow Dodge convertible up here registered in his name and his father's worth two and a half million. Oil. But old Pablo has to go through the Corps. Make a man of him.

While we started getting into our uniforms, the sound-off rat bellowed in the hall to rouse the upperclassmen on the floors above. "First call to chow, sirs! Raincoats, sirs!" Everyone down the line groaned because if it didn't rain we'd swelter in the bleachers under the coat plus the high-button blouse and wool pants. Once in the dress for the day, there was no backing out; you stayed in it. By 6:35 sharp the menu was being shouted: "Scrambled eggs, bacon, toast and jelly, sirs!" And it was Inspection Call. Mike's the slaphappy kind. Can't keep a poker face like me to save himself.

The upperclassman stalked in with a big smile. "Brace," he squealed, "I want to see fifty-four wrinkles in your chins!" He squatted to get a look into Mike's belt buckle, rubbing his stubble. "Rat, I got a wart here on my chin, ain't I? There's one showing up in your brass mirror here."

Mike started to giggle. He couldn't help it. "No, sir."

"Now I want you to polish that, mister. I don't like warts."

"Yes, sir," Mike croaked, chin-bone flat against his Adam's apple and brown eyes popping.

"Did he laugh? Did that rat laugh!" The Big Man wheeled to look at me duplicating Mike's posture.

"If you say he did, sir," I wheezed in a bass tone, which is what happens to me when my throat gets squeezed and my neck aches, "why he certainly did."

By now Mike couldn't chain his smile any more. They've got a name for him too: Ape. He's happy-happy. "Wipe that grin off, mister!" Mike made the motion, using his hand as directed. "Now dig a hole and bury it." Mike went through those gestures as if he had a spade. "Whistle taps over it, Ape!" Mike tried, puckering up in a grimace to keep back his giggles.

When the upperclassman finally got through with this nutty act and sailed away, Mike groaned. "You think A. Lincoln could have gone through that and still kept his funny bone? And I've got to cheer all afternoon, too."

I thumped his shoulder fondly. "Who cares? We'll be out of here tonight. To think I can forget your face for six whole days."

"Say, how do you feel about going home, Jason?" Mike was dead sober all of a sudden.

"I don't know. Dad says everybody's crazy about her."

The sound-off was at it again, and they marched us over to the mess hall for breakfast. You weren't required to eat the chow though, so we broke line and went back to our hole to clean it up and to pack. Our wastebaskets have to be turned over, steel sinks shining and dried out, blanket corners mitered. I had some peanut butter in the bottom of a jar I'd bought a month ago, and Mike had part of a loaf of white bread that wasn't more than ten days old. We made a meal of it, spreading the stuff with a toothbrush handle.

"Guaranteed to glue your teeth together," Mike said in authentic Ape style. "Feed it to your mother-in-law to keep her trap shut."

"Use it to plug leaks," I joined in, "or hang wallpaper. Or lay asphalt tile in your gala new playroom!"

"Yeah." Mike put the empty jar in his drawer under the socks in order not to mess up the wastebasket. He looked me up and down. "No fooling, Jewel. You're worrying."

"Who me?"

"You've been a foggy man all morning."

I sat down on the cot edge. I didn't care if it got wrinkled; you can keep all that crap. "Wish my old lady wasn't dead." I shook my head like a lost baby "It hit her that quick, Mike. One spring she noticed the littlest lump under the arm. She didn't go see a doctor till June. The next spring she was out like a light. She had the whitest skin you ever saw, my mother, and red hair like silk." I couldn't stop my slippery tongue. "I never think of her the way she got at the end. Skinny and yellowish. Kind of absent with me. Dad quit work and turned the paper over to a friend of his. He couldn't believe it either. Her eyes were greenish; she had dimples in her cheeks when she smiled." I could feel I'd talked enough and managed to clam up.

Mike was staring at me. "You going to call *her* Mother?"

"No." My dad had written me, *I hope you'll see fit to extend to her all your courtesy.* The dumb dame, I thought. And you dog. I couldn't stand the idea. "Don't know what I'm going home for, Mike. Sure don't."

"Come with me then, Jason! My folks won't care. We've got plenty of room. You'd like my kid sister. She's fourteen. La-de-dah!" He was grinning. Plain you couldn't have kept him from his family.

"No. It is for me to do." I sounded theatrical. *Listen well. I will do what I must do. I will try harder than I have tried before in all of my life.* "Got to see my old man anyway, Mike. No mon, no fun, your son."

"How sad, too bad, your dad!" Mike worked part time in the mess hall kitchen which gave him an independence. He'd been working in his home town too, for the past four or five summers, so he was paying his own tuition. Maybe that's why he didn't make cracks about his folks. Dad frowned on my earning a nickel at Tech. *Any free time you have, son, you spend on boning, hear? I'd like the Corps to remember you. Let me know if your account runs short.*

My dad's something of a character, big-boned, gray-haired, jowly. He owns this little paper, the Ordinary Bend *Sentinel.* He was given some award last year for a series of editorials he wrote. I don't know what on, schools or Indians or Negroes or hospitals. And he's a buller. *Tye Weston, raconteur,* is the way the *Sentinel* always puts it. He's famous for that habit clear over to L.A. and back to New York. He'd even bulled himself into a new wife, hadn't he?

Don't get the idea I don't like my dad. We always got along okay. But somewhere between my growing from eleven to seventeen he changed. From the Great Giver of Goodies, the Big Funny Man, he transformed into the Tedious Moralizer, the Humorless Sanctified Dad of Today. Probably my fault more than his. I'm pretty single-minded; lean toward my own ideas. And he has this notion of molding a Man out of a Boy. He's been carrying on about Old Corps since I was old enough to listen. We'd drive up to Tech's games, five hundred miles, ever since I was six. When I got brains enough to get a glimmering of what goes on with football, I said I'd rather stay home. Then even a true Jewel, I was writing a mystery for the school yearbook. But the Great I Am stood on one leg and howled, so off to the game we went. When I came up here a couple of months ago he tooted his final sermon into my ears. *Make them remember you, boy.* Balls.

Anyway, looks like he got lonely after I left home; he took someone in to warm his toes. I don't blame him. My mother's been dead three years. He flew to the west coast on a lecture tour. There he renewed old acquaintances, I guess. Popped the question. Made me feel like throwing up. But now I was broke again. Money goes past me as though it's greased. In eight weeks I've earned lasting fame as the easiest touch in our barracks. I hate to spend his money that way. Going to ask him to cancel my account here and mail little checks instead. I figure that way I'll not be tempted.

For the Ape's benefit I forced a laugh. "It is for me to do!"

Mike gave me a push in the chest and we scrabbled around a little. Then we finished packing and before you knew it, the orderly was bawling in the hall again, "All freshmen out!" We snapped to it. By three in the afternoon I was peeling off my

My Old Lady

raincoat and the shower was still flowing down as I climbed into Soliel's convertible, voice like a bullfrog. There were six of us, our spit-polished shoes mud-daubed, pants damp and creaseless.

"We look sweet," Pablo warbled as he took the wheel, "like drowning rats!" He was a Spanish type, black-haired. I envied him his ease at driving. One-handed, doing ninety lots of the time, he didn't make a miscalculation; I watched close. He set me down on Oak Street a little after ten, which is an average of seventy. And we had dropped two other cadets off along the way, too. You had to admire it. "See you, Jewel," he yodeled, "Tuesday. Ten on the dot."

As he gunned off, I picked up my grip. I walked down Ash Street and up to the house. It's big and spare and there's a porch in front. The windows were all lit up. I shivered as if I were nearing the skirt barn at Cresthill School; only there you had a fighting chance. You might be in your ducks; white gloves, white cross belts, inspected to a fare-thee-well; and the girl's sporting a hat the way they make them do, and heels. You're cold strangers. But you have a chance.

From the wet sidewalks steam fogged up, making the lights blur from the houses up the street. I got the creeps. What was I doing here? Wished I'd taken Mike up; I wouldn't mind that la-de-dah sister. I felt I'd been away a year, not a couple of months. The house looked shabby and small, the paved walk-way short. The wind smelled the way it did when I was a little kid, like honey, the dark kind from locust blooms. Wet dying leaves were everywhere.

I was turning over inside. Once the Great Giver of Goodies used to take me down to Jake Loudon's general store with him. He'd go about getting his stuff. I'd stare at the men's legs walking around, sometimes catch my dad's through the others, wrinkled khakis, lumberjacket over the thighs. I wouldn't stir, never looking up.

In a rush I was down the walk and up the steps. There was laughter inside. I looked through the window. Dad had his back to the open fire, bulling it. I knew most of the folks there, one or two young ones. I figured the party was for her. I opened the door, giving it a big swing, not meaning to, and it clattered as it hit the wall in back. Dad stopped in the middle of a sentence and then was lunging over to hug me and clap me on the shoulders. He took my bag and was trying to pull my cap out of my hands. I held on to it instinctively because it had all my papers under the visor. Finally it reached my brain that this was a close relative of mine and it would be safe with him. I guess I was acting pretty crazy. All I remember is, in a little while I was sitting in the easy chair in the corner and Emily Grossett was on the footstool feeding me popcorn with her lily-like, sixteen-year-old hands.

"Emily," I said, chewing, and hearing my dad going off at the mouth, "this is sure swell. Haven't had popcorn since I left Oklahoma."

She nodded. "Want some fudge, too, Jason? I'd like you to know I think your uniform's dreamy."

"Needs pressing, don't you think? And look at my shoes." I was testing her, and Emily came forth with an A.

"I don't see anything wrong, Jason. You're just dreamy!"

Then I saw *her* across the room. There was never anyone like that in Ordinary Bend. She was mixing a drink at the sideboard. Must have been a size eight, with a trim figure. She had a dress on that made her stand out like a fresh rat in a crack drill. I didn't go for it a bit. Emily, now, was wearing something frothy white like whipped cream, and the townswomen looked respectable, skirts down around their calves, bows and pins on, or a black velvet ribbon. Earrings and beads too. But you should have seen her. No jewelry; and this dress fit like skin and was cut off short at her little knees. Her gray hair was combed up in some oddball way. Who did she think she was? Some French queen? She handed me a half-smile. I thought I'd get some of whatever they were drinking.

"I'll be back, Emily honey." I stumbled over the footstool

getting up. I thought I'd extend to her my courtesy like her husband had suggested.

She was solemn as an owl. "What'll you have, sir?"

"Mister. I'm still a cadet." I was blushing the way I get in class when they send me up in front to explain. It isn't that I don't know what I'm going to say, or that I give a crap for any one of those guys sitting there. But I have to blush. There I stood like the queen of the May. "What you got, lady?"

"Let's say a glass of sherry?"

Like I'm some old granny. "Thanks, but I'll take a martini like yours."

"All right, mister." Cool as grass, smiley as an old royal *madame*, she mixed and handed it to me. "Nice to meet you at last, Jason. I hear a lot about you."

I slugged half the drink like a movie detective and felt my blush leaving. I was a rock again. "You're some piece of lace." I hoped my dad didn't overhear. "What's he got you want, lady?" My manhood was raring up now. All my lonely days and crying nights, all that dimpled face and red hair like running water, all the resentment at the change time wrought in the little boy's Funny Man. I took it out on her. It rolled into a ball somewhere below my belt and I thought I'd get rid of it in one big thrust. And the gin wasn't slowing me down any. Or the stale room or the fire's heat.

"You better drink that a trifle slower. Hmm?" Her red mouth turned up at the corners but it wasn't a smile. She looked a little scared and put her hand on my arm, shushing with her lips.

Then my dad was there too, bulldog face in a frown. "Well well, the two of you making up for lost time?" He was mighty hearty. "Jason, your old teacher, Mrs. Hawkins, has been telling me all the ladies admire this little woman. But they say she's setting too high a standard for the other wives!"

I turned away from them. My brain was in a spin, and I knew

Children and Lovers

I was going to make an all-American ass of myself in a minute. I was dead too, awake before sound-off, throat raw from yelping in the rain earlier. I managed to make it over to Emily and lowered myself into the chair.

I must have fallen asleep then, because the next thing I remember is opening my eyes in the dark and nobody being there. The fire was a glare of coals across the room. Dad was coming in and helping me out of the chair and up the stairs. He didn't say a word, guided me into my room and went out, shutting the door. I pursed my mouth, swaying, and listened for the key to turn because I'd been such a bad, bad boy. But the only sound was him padding down the hall to the queen's bed. I stood in the dark feeling sorry for myself and letting hate for my old man go snaking through me the way it did when I was eleven and he made me go to that game.

Near noon I woke. Sometime in the night, I'd dragged off my clothes and they were lying around. I was under the cool sheet in my birthday suit, feeling great. My subconscious must have been working at it because I knew exactly what I was going to do. There's this three-hundred-some acres Mr. Bledsoe, a friend of my dad's, has outside Ordinary Bend where the first mountain range begins. I used to camp there a lot, alone or with one of my scout buddies. I needed some fresh air. Every human I knew stunk.

My quick anger made me come up out of bed in a jump. I was pulling things out of drawers and the closet. I got down my gun, a little single-shot Winchester. It shoots low; I know every fault it has. I cleaned it to be sure, though it didn't need it. Then I got down my bedroll and put extra socks and a heavy sweater in it, and my camp cooking outfit. I let my rat uniform lie on the floor; I'd been pressing seams and polishing brass too long. I put the gun in my roll and tied it up snug. I was still naked.

There was a rap at the door. "Come right in!" I was yearning to see the bit of lace. "Dahling," I cried, arms et cetera extended. Her little face, with that Frenchy hairdo, spooked in and out and the door slapped shut. I stifled a yelp of delight.

When I was dressed in my old cits and lacing up my boots, I felt fine, not a bit like an anxious Corps bootlicker. I slid my knife case onto the well-worn belt and fastened the dingy buckle. I stuffed my near-depleted billfold in my pocket, slung my jacket over my arm and grabbed the bedroll. It hefted light enough. There was no one on the stairway, and I slipped into the kitchen. There I unbuttoned my shirt and stuffed some things into it and my pockets: matches, a can opener, half a pound of margarine, some bacon, a sack of rice, shakers of salt and pepper. I ripped a sheet off the pad hanging on the wall. "Camping on Deer Hill a few days," I scribbled and left it on the counter. I was out the back door and around the side of the house and down the walk. My luck didn't hold.

"Jason, where the hell?" I glanced back to see Dad in the front doorway, a tablet of yellow paper clutched in one hand.

"Going up to Bledsoe's, Dad," I yelled, too loud. "I'll check in with him." I rushed on. Don't know if I thought he was going to charge after me or what. But I felt purged and not lonely any more. Let him come! On the road out of Ordinary Bend, I stopped in at Jake Loudon's and got a hunting license and laid in some more stores. Untying the bedroll, I dumped the stuff from my shirt in with the rest. Three loaves of country rye, canned beans, sack of apples, a few oranges.

"How's school, youngster? Home on vacation, huh? See old man Weston now and then. *Sentinel's* not a bad paper." Jake rattled on. He's simple to satisfy with a grunt or nod. I couldn't pay for all I got and asked him to put some of it on account. Guessed I'd settle that with Dad too when I got back, if we were on speaking terms. I tramped out of town whistling.

What a day! The sun sat up there, brassy. Birds hollered like mad; one cardinal clanged in the top of a sycamore, *"What cheer! Chuck chuck chuck chuck chuck!"* I snuffled like a buck

deer and began to trot, about to jump out of my skin. Must
have run five miles till I slowed. About half way I'd got my
second wind, which always gives me a thrill. Sounds pretty
corny, but I get this feeling I could fly if I really wanted. Not
that I was going to test myself; I'm too bright for that.

"Eeee-yow!" I paced up the steep grade into the hills. The
blue jays honked down at me.

I opened the gate to Mr. Bledsoe's place, which is posted. I
went up to the lodge, and he gave me the okay to stay out on
Deer Hill. He said there'd been plenty of feed so far this fall,
and the deer were fat and staying back in the timber. I kept to
the stream past a pond or two and had some trouble finding the
trail. Been two years since I'd camped there last, but I lit on it
after a while. By the time I was picking out a camp site it was
pretty late. I'd forgot my watch, left it on the dresser, but the
sun was down. I set up on the edge of an open field on the east
side of the mountain, not far from water. Dry and high up. It
looked off to the granite ranges, bluish in the east where Arkan-
sas lay.

I broke pine boughs and made a place to spread my bedroll
and gathered a stack of dry sticks and logs. I'd quieted by then.
I heated a can of beans in the coals and ate them with a couple
of winesaps. Then I crawled into my roll while twilight floated
over like a hovering bird. I belonged here; this was home. My
feet warmed, and it spread all through me. I took long breaths
of the pitch scent from the crushed pine under me. An owl
roused me, "Huh-hoo-hoo-hoo-huh-hhh!" It plunged nearby;
there was a tiny squeak, and it was winging across me, brushing
its soft feathers, silhouetted against the open sky. I turned over.

When I woke again, the world was on fire. By the time the
sun labored up through it, all the colors were pale, and I had a
fire going. Bacon sputtered in a pan; I was over at a deep spot I
knew in the creek, on my stomach trying to snare a trout. I
didn't have a reel, only a line and a hook with a cricket drowning on it. The water was a mirror, and the trout moved slug-

gishly on the bottom. In time I flipped out three small ones, which I cleaned and dropped beside the bacon. Must have taken me an hour to finish that meal, taking each bite slow and easy, lolled against some old oak roots. I remembered the peanut butter. *Feed it to your mother-in-law to glue her trap shut,* my old lady'd said. I was all loosened up, beginning to regret my manners to the *madame*. My technique had been on a two-year-old level. Don't know why, but I get carried away sometimes like a gun fired wild, so I miss the target altogether.

I spent five days on Deer Hill. All that time I saw no one but Mr. Bledsoe once, out after poachers, riding an apple-nosed bay gelding. It stood rooted when he dropped the lines and ambled over. "Tye phoned up. Wants to know what day you plan on getting into Ordinary Bend." I told him Monday. We shot the breeze a while. Mr. Bledsoe has a problem with illegal hunters; last fall he came on six does shot and crippled up some way so he had to finish them off and bury them. One year he even located a wounded antelope. I waited till he left to think about it, wondering how my dad was taking it. He might not like my missing Thanksgiving. I hadn't asked Mr. Bledsoe if he sounded mad. I didn't care really.

One afternoon an old skunk went down the trail followed by half a dozen babies in a string. That evening I shot a gray squirrel for supper. Largest I ever saw, a male. After skinning and gutting and quartering him, I fried bacon pieces and rice together and put the squirrel with it. I added a little water and salt and plenty of pepper and dropped the lid on. I lay back and let it go till night, being hungry but not in a lather. Smelling the smoke and the cooking, and watching dusk come to dark.

The air was so quiet, I could hear the stream muttering, flowing down the side of Deer Hill. The wind coasted up from the valley, hard, the way it will do in April, as if it's come from a distance. And smelling like that purple candy you get in some movie houses. Sad too; not funeral sad, where somebody's lost and you can't bear it. More as if there's a thing you knew before you came into this world, and you can almost recollect it. Not quite. The next day and the next I spent waiting for it to come to me. The breeze charged up, and I sprawled in the grass watching the sky, trying to see behind the blue. If there were a few clouds, I tried to stare through them.

I went tramping along the trails and on the cushioned forest floor. Mostly there are oak and pine, a climax stand, self-perpetuating. That's the way all forests in America once were, and the plains too, where grass roots lay eight feet deep and more. That was before the *men-with-faces-painted-white* came through chock full of hot poop on how to make a desert of a rich land.

Deer Hill was high and clean of trees where I'd camped; there were no shadows until the very bottom. That's why it was so startling when I got back late one afternoon and the meadow was full of deer, bluish-gray coats getting heavy, black-tip tails hanging relaxed, mule ears forward as they cropped. I stayed clutching my gunstock till my wrist ached. The sun fell and the west sky acted like a rainbow. The blacktails began to move toward the creek for water, stepping up a few at a time. Two were playing, bucks with forked antlers; white bellies flashing, they reared and pawed each other the way horses do. A yearling doe finished drinking and trotted briskly up the bank. She put her head sideways and flicked her tail so her white flag stood up; she shot in the air in a dizzy bound which spooked the whole lot. They scampered down the field like a band of hares and disappeared in the forest.

I sighed, and managed to move toward stacking the fire. I broke a loaf of heavy country rye into hunks and put them on a stick to toast. Slapping on margarine, I wolfed them. I crawled into my sack; Venus flickered and went out and came back brighter than before. Later, in a start, I rose out of my blanket thinking the forest was on fire in the east. It was the low squashed moon, a burning blood-orange. After a while it broke free of the earth to float high, round and white.

My Old Lady

In the morning there were tracks on the creek bank and deer turd marbles all over the place. On the other side of where I had my line dropped in the trout hole, a young fox came slipping in the grass, looking up now and then at the jays that were screeching at him. He kept yawning, closing his button eyes and opening his jaws wide. Shiny red, leg-fur sleek and black. At dusk that day, when the fire was in coals, I heard his bark, husky and weird, half a snarl. The nighthawks were up in a flock, booming as they hurled down and rose abruptly in mid-flight, catching insects. A woodmouse slid out from his hole beneath the root where I sat. He reared on his haunches, pointed nose sniffing. I ran my hand out softly and had him. By the waning light, his coat was thick and long and golden-fawn above, whiter than ermine under. After I toyed with him a while, I placed him back. He licked his paws quickly and brushed his hair forward like a cat cleaning himself. He stared at me, black eyes reflecting the coals, and slunk under the root once more. It was my last night, and I turned in too.

After breakfast, I took my time breaking camp, scouring the pan and utensils with creek sand, shaking out my clothes before folding them in the bedroll and tying it together. The sun was overhead when I left the spot, hating to go. Wished I could stay on Deer Hill till Resurrection Day. I'd make out Indian style, maybe. But then I thought how Red Men lived by codes too. Guiding natural spirits had to give them their names through inspired loco-dreams that meant something or other. And they were true blue, the Indians. Yeah. Honor bright, to their way of thinking. Just like my Corps and its honor formula. Gentlemen didn't cheat steal or lie; every cadet was a gentleman. Balls they were. Far as I could make out all those systems when men got together were full of corn. I felt raceless and colorless. I'd make a good hermit.

But for all my fancy thinking, here I was heading down the side of the range toward my destiny. As they say. I stopped in to thank Mr. Bledsoe, who was glad to hear the deer were down.

Children and Lovers

Then I was on the road. I stripped off my bulky sweater and tied it around my waist by the sleeves. The birds were still whooping it up in the tops of trees. I didn't listen. Too busy hardening myself. At sunset, I passed the town limit sign. I clumped up the walkway, across which dead leaves scudded, collecting on the lawn. The wind burst in fits and starts; the sky was gray and undecided.

My old man was opening the front door. He grunted, "Jason. You're back."

I sprinted up the stairs to him, awkward. "Hullo, Dad!"

"How was it up there?"

"Great."

"That's good."

"Yeah. Saw a big herd of blacktails. Mr. Bledsoe had figured they were still high in the timber. And a family of skunks, too. And a cub fox, a red one. And you know that old trout hole? There's a mess of them in there this fall. I fried up a few." I was being a genuine Jewel, sparkling. When my tongue gets slippery, I can't stop it. I knew it was no time to be running off like that, and I reeled in desperately.

"Can I talk to you about money?"

"In here."

My dad's built like a bear, and he's just about as expression-less. You never can tell what's going on behind those bonny blue eyes. He might be about to laugh or about to bite some-one's head off. He was heading for his office in back of the living room, where he writes his pieces. The building where the *Sentinel's* put together by the staff is up on Oak Street. I dropped my gear in the hall and followed. My flanks were wet under the heavy sweater, and my armpits. Way I was acting, you'd think my dad was some steel-ball strict guy, some Corps wheel that had caught me lousing up the Code of Honor. And I was to be drummed out for it. While we walked the length of flooring to his room, I screwed my mind on that midnight. They'd routed us from the sack in the rain and paraded us to

---

My Old Lady

the lower quadrangle. There they rolled the drums and the Regimental Commander faintly yelled orders. Like some odd-ball dream. We were marched back soaking and silent. Already my stride was changing, and I was squaring corners. I sat in a chair at a brace, tucking in my chin. He fixed his eyes on me.

"Well, son? We missed you for the Thanksgiving party. I wanted you at home but Ruth said to let you go. We'd like you to enjoy your leave, don't intend to be selfish. She insisted you need to try your legs out. The weather was fine, wasn't it? Now what's the matter? Money? You're not broke already."

"I certainly am, sir." I rubbed my thumbs together, miserable. "Even went and put some stuff on your account at Jake Loudon's."

"But I deposited a hundred to your name at Tech three weeks ago. You wrote that it was too much."

"I know. It was. But somehow it went. I was thinking, Dad, if you'd close that account and send me a little now and then, I'd spend a lot less. Maybe I'd learn."

"Want *me* to do your thinking for you, Jason? In the Old Corps an extra hundred like that'd last a year. Well, I take in more than my old man did too, I suppose. You're going to have to teach yourself to curb yourself. Soft boy! Don't you know, *the man who can accomplishes more than ten who must?*" There was a lot more of the same, like: *a wagon goes the way the horse pulls it;* and *ready with your cap but slow with your purse.* The Sanctified Moralizer scampered away in top form, finally mentioning his hopes for me, that I'd get the scholastic ribbon and more besides. Then he picked up some papers from the desk and fumbled for a pencil. His eyes sort of skinned over the way a bird'll do. He looked at me as though I'd just entered the room. "Dinner at six-thirty, son."

I didn't square any corners leaving. Snatched my roll and ducked up the stairs. The room had been gone over but good since I'd left. Swept and tidied. I opened the closet door and my uniform hung cleaned and pressed. I decided the dame was

pretty cagey. After I'd showered and shaved, I got into my gray
pants and shirt and black four-in-hand. I posed in the mirror;
real dillberry, all dressed up and nowhere to go. I was feeling
sick to my stomach; I intended to be *very* careful. At precisely
one minute before half-past six, I left the room.

The meal started out an *after you, Alfonse* comedy, everyone
being too polite about the food to last. Dad carved the roast, his
eyebrows raised. She asked, "Won't you have some salad,
Jason?" and never batted an eye. Her hair was combed up in
place and she was wearing a gray sort of dress, as short as the
other night, but this one buttoned high at the neck. She looked
older, some way. They were arguing on town politics and tossed
it back and forth for a while. I was too bothered to pay attention but it had to do with the school board election. All at once
she turned to me. "But we shouldn't go into this tonight, Tye.
We're leaving the boy out!"

"Well, Jason." He dug into his plate.

She started putting questions to me about the Corps, and I
told her what I could, easing up some. But then Dad began
interrupting to set me straight. It made me jumpy as a coot.
When she asked what eating square was I figured I'd try out
some corny wit. "Decline to answer on the grounds it could
incinerate me," I flashed.

She laughed at that. "You don't have to tell, Jason. I must
sound like a House committee."

For some reason that made the Tedious Humorless Dad of
Today get red as a rose. No sir, she was going to comprehend
what it was at once, "You put your feet like this, Ruth. See?
And your back like this. It's a ramrod! And you spear your food
and then you start squaring, see? It goes like—"

I couldn't tolerate him. Getting up, I threw my napkin in the
middle of my plate. "Can't you see how stupid you make me
look?" I was near tears. I could have hit him that moment.

"Jason!" he protested. "Son."

"You old man," I yelled, "let me off the hook. I'm not going through your *Old Corps*. Get it? Tech's different now. There's new jazz added every year. You bull along all the while about A. Lincoln, how he was cramming and boning at *my* age. Well, what was A. Lincoln doing at *your* age! Tell me that. Why don't you find out what *I* think sometime? Another thing, I hate football. Always have. Only go because somebody makes me." I was sobbing like some drunken goon. "Next year I won't have to attend, and you know what? I'll never see another football field till they tuck me under the grass. You old—!"

I'd been shouting helplessly. I sped from the room, upstairs to the dark where I closed my door. As I dashed, I seemed to stand aside to watch this spindle-shank howling and galloping about. I thought, *Is that me? Well, at least you finally shut up the champion buller of forty-nine states.* He'd been open-mouthed as a spitted frog.

While I cooled, I began to feel the first prickle of shame. And so, deliberately I dived into a lake of hate. Lying on the bed, stretching my limbs, I stared up at blackness. My mouth got dry. I kept veering about, considering. Seventeen and roped and tied. Everything was nutty. I circled in that lake until I slowed into sleep.

I opened my eyes. The room was half-lit by moonlight streaming in. For an instant, I was in my roll at Deer Hill. Then I saw her standing at the iron bed-rail at the foot. She was looking away, out of the window at the moon, her hand fingering the neckline of her dress. She glanced down at my shoes and bent over to unlace them; she slipped them off. I held my breath, because my mother used to do that.

"Hullo, lady."

"Jason?" She sat on the bed beside me, leaning down to loosen my tie.

"He's mighty set on molding a Man out of a Boy." I took the tie from her hands and slid it off and unbuttoned my shirt collar. "My mother never rode me. She wasn't any more like him than I am."

Children and Lovers

"She wasn't?"

"When she got sick, she couldn't stand for people to find out. Dad had to warn our relatives not to call up on the phone any oftener than they'd used to, so she wouldn't catch on they knew. I tried to act as if she were just like always. Sometimes I think I'm beginning to forget her. Afraid I will. Her eyes were greenish." I shook my head slowly. "Guess I'm pretty crazy, the way I've been acting to you."

"No."

"Really jumped on Dad tonight. That dumb cornball."

"Don't you feel a bit sorry for him? You're hard on Tye. Everything's behind your father, you see. And it's all starting for you." She was a ghost, hair blue-white in that moonlight. And her mouth pale, her hand moving at her throat like a trout on the bottom.

"Sorry I'm so stupid. I like your hair and the way it is."

"I can see through Tye like a glass. I know most of his faults. Couldn't you try a little to understand him? It takes such patience, I know, at your age. But in a special way, your father's a great man, Jason."

"Yeah."

"Nobody's perfect."

"I know."

"Say Ruth if you like."

I was sleepy, and her hand touched like cool water on my cheek. She unfolded the extra quilt to spread it over me. When I awoke in a few minutes, she wasn't there.

Pablo Soliel was right on time. Ten to the dot. The weather was turning, and snow was predicted. We blasted out of town, and I spent the next few hours betting on the Spaniard's skill with that yellow roadster. Never expected it'd feel so good to get back to our barracks hole. Looked all fine and cozy. I was down polishing the last corner of the floor, which I'd coated with wax, when my old lady arrived. He stood in the doorway, Ape face all in a wide grin, the skirts of his Corps overcoat sweeping low. His gear was in one hand, a long bundle under his arm.

"Slick," I told him. "So step easy."

"Brought a new rug with me, Jewel." Mike tossed the package on his cot and unbuttoned his coat. He flung it aside.

"Great." I got up from my knees.

"Tell me the news." He was ripping the string and rattling the brown paper. "How was it at home?"

"She's not so bad, Mike. I call her Ruth now."

We spread the rug down, and it made our hole look rather toney.

The Daemon

She watched the gray bird from the window overlooking her back view. He had arrived yesterday. The white bars of his wings and tail flashed as he darted and circled in angry pursuit. She wondered where he had come from, why this daemon was in him to harass her birds. The brooding sky of November shook a chill rain into the clearing bordered in the rear by tall black cherry trees. She loved the back yard. The cherries screened the neighbor houses and in summer they gathered close, spreading branches like green arms about her sanctuary. The two bird stations were near the middle of the lawn, next to the little pear tree, one at a distance from the other so the gentler shyer birds could retreat a little if they wished. And she always spread grain freely on the grass for doves and ground birds. The young redbird was winging in. She had watched the parent-bird feed him from her stands all the summer. But now the gray mockingbird cried out in a burring sound and fluttered at him, attacking. The redbird sped silent to perch in the high tree-limbs and to wonder at this unwonted violence.

"Oh, no," she murmured. "He's but a baby. You're a bad bird, you mocker." It was like an undigested thing in her, so heavy. "He's such a baby, and where can he feed but here?" He had learned to come to her yard. The old red male had taught him, the two lighting out there all last summer, the parent

163

giving a sunflower seed and then cracking one for himself. The red baby was greedy and would spread his wings, begging to be fed again. Every night and every morning they'd been out there. Bewildered now, he was watching from the top of the tree. Then the mockingbird flew high at him, and the red flashed away.

In the mornings she liked to bring her tea and Danish to this window and count her birds. She kept a log and each day would write the numbers of each kind, and if a new one arrived make a wavering pencil line below, welcoming it. But today she had no appetite, not even for the weak tea she'd brewed. And the yard was emptied. Early she had awakened, pushing back the covers. She had shoved her bony feet into her slippers and pulled her gray wrapper about her, shuffling to this window. In the half-light the form had been there, shrouded, hunched in the lower branches of the small pear tree by the stands.

Rain had begun to fall. She had dressed and tugged on boots and scooped grain into a pan as was her custom. She put on the mackinaw that had been her husband's and still hung on the kitchen coat-tree. She staggered into the yard, in the slight drizzle. The bird remained in the tree while she scattered grain. It eyed her, head cocked, the one black button brittle. "Huh," she cried. "Scat!" It hopped to a higher branch. A sharp rage caught her and she clutched the slender tree trunk to shake it, the pan clattering to the ground so the rest of the grain sprinkled on the wetness. Still the gray bird clung, swaying in an upper limb. She reached her tiny-boned arms up, snatched at the branches, clucking angrily at him. Silently then he winged off. "You stay away now!" She was half-crying, breathing the damp air spasmodically.

She stumbled to the house, from the window saw that the gaudy tribe of jays, blue and cheerful, were already arriving. They were coming back. Her joy leaped. A sparrow came, one, three, more. But no. There was the flash of gray, white-barred, sweeping here and there. Then he perched on the stand alone, shaking his wings, triumphant. He pecked at the seed, his sticks of legs outspread. She went to make her tea, but had not the heart for a roll. And how could she bear to sit in the chair at the window?

"I must think what to do about this," she whispered into the empty kitchen. One of the wood cabinets in the room was broken, and the house seemed crumbling about her. Since he had died there was no one to do things, and through disuse and lack of repair, the place was mouldering and dying. Only the window was alive. The back view and the bright sweet birds.

That evening the rain lifted and the sun broke for a moment through heavy clouds, a ball white and luminous, almost like the moon. She was heating a bowl of soup for supper when she heard him caroling wildly, lilting. She ran to the window. He was in the top branch of the little pear tree, dominant over the world she had created for her flocks of birds. His fine song held terror for her. She knew he was proclaiming for all the feathered wild to heed that this was his own, to hold. To rule alone.

Yet more purely he sang, and never such clever variations. Exultant, lusty; then hear, how tender and soft! Distracted, she ran out without stopping for boots or coat, to gather stones by the house-side, bending her obstinate joints. "Oh, go away!" She hurled the stones and they fell short. But the song had been stopped. He was flying to the tall trees out of range, and yet her feeble arms pitched the rest of the rocks, which fell on the grass. He watched, impassive, and she felt how he had conquered. The clearing was his! She returned to the house, where a burned odor told her that the soup had boiled away and the pan was ruined.

A day or so later the paper boy came to collect. "What's wrong, missus?" He had noticed her paleness. "You getting the flu?" He was her friend and sometimes she allowed him to come to the window to see her flocks. Last summer he had watched the young redbird being fed apple bits by its father.

The Daemon

"There is a bad bird in my yard," she said. "Come, I will show you."

"He thinks he's Napoleon," the boy said.

"He won't go away," she worried aloud. "The birds are used to feeding here. They've forgot how to hunt berries in the wild. He won't let them eat, you see."

"He's got delusions of grandeur," the boy shouted, as the bird swooped after a mourning dove that had come fluttering, crying in staccato greeting as it landed. The dove flew up, awkward, routed from the yard.

She murmured. "There. A dove is stupid, you know. It will starve. Poor thing."

"Say, I could build a trap, missus. For the wicked one."

"A trap?"

"With a neat door that slid down. Bang! And a string to the window for you to pull."

"No," she told him, her face like a withered leaf. "No, I couldn't trap a bird. He is free."

"Well, then," the boy said. "I must get at my collecting."

She followed him to the door, saying, "I had an idea to move one of the stands out to the front yard." But he had gone while she stood there muttering. A plan was forming in her mind. How simple. Of course. While the mocker was guarding the back yard the birds could feed in front. Even he could be in only one place at a time. She chuckled.

Pulling on the man's heavy jacket, she went into the yard. She gripped one of the heavy stands and, hauling sometimes, and again shoving, maneuvered it around the house. She panted and whimpered, stopping now and then to get breath. "Hee! I'll fool him one time. Hee." When the stand was set up in the front yard, which faced the old suburban street, she took feed and crusts of bread and a spoonful of peanut butter to entice them there. Soon sparrows were gathering. She saw them as she peered out from the edge of the front parlor curtains. Night was draping cold and purple over the outside world. She'd foiled him!

She slept well, smiling in the dark of her side of the big white bed that she'd occupied alone for the past few years. Ever since he had died. She was glad he was gone though, because the pain had been constant in the last months and he'd wanted to be done with living. She was never lonely; she had the birds. In the summer she'd take a chair into the yard. They were not afraid of her and swarmed about.

While she was sleeping, a snowfall began. Large flakes settled soundless on the slanted roof and made collars on the pear-tree limbs and tall mounds on the two bird stations, in back and in front. She took her breakfast tea and Danish to the window seat, anticipating some excitement. A few sparrows were out there, scratching in the snow after the feed she had thrown. Then they were flying up all at once, scattering like blown cinders before a streak of plunging gray.

She spilled the hot tea as she set the cup down and pulled at the chair-arms to get to her feet. She hurried to the front parlor curtain. There, too, like an avenging angel, the bird was swooping, driving starlings and jays before him. Then he disappeared. She realized he was in the snow-bank atop the roof, on guard, all-seeing, omnipotent.

She was no longer hungry. The unhappy anger, the frustration, were hot in her, and her fingers shook.

The wind blustered all that day and in the early dark she was yet at the window. Now if a bird or two came, she would whimper, "Fight. Fight him back." Clenching her fingers. "Eat quickly. Eat! Before he comes, while he's busy on the other side." A sparrow was feeding in the snow when, like an eagle on a lamb, the mocker struck. The pair were fluttering in a white drift. "He's killing it," she cried. "Murderer!" Rapping on the window. The gray wings beat, outspreading over the prostrate bit of brown.

The Daemon

"Daemon!" She ran to the door, unheeding her flimsy shoes, out in the snow. The struggling birds flew up and away. She halted. "I'm acting a loony." She looked down at herself and hurried back into the house. "What am I doing?" She raised her dampened skirts, gazing at her wet skinny legs. Dazed she took off the shoes and pulled the long soaked stockings from her feet.

When she had changed her clothes, she waited until the morning paper came. Thwack! It hit the doorstep. She was there in an instant, surprising quick. "Boy! Come. Come here."

"Yes, missus?"

"Have a cup of milk." She drew him in. "Here's a sweet cracker."

He was willing, stamping snow from his boots, blowing on red rough hands.

"You spoke of a trap? To catch that naughty bird," she questioned.

"You want one? Sure." He was pleased, businesslike. He strode to the window. "See there?" He pointed, dropping crumbs, but she didn't mind. "I'd run a wire. I've thought about it." His face grew alive with his idea. "I have an electro-magnet from an old train set. I'll fix it so all you need do is touch a button and you'll have him."

"When can you bring it?"

"This afternoon? I'll do it."

And he kept his word. She watched his burly body move about in the snow-draped clearing. The day was brightening, the sky bluing. The mockingbird, disturbed, had vanished. She knew he was peeking from somewhere back in the trees, wondering. "Let him puzzle this one out." She wagged her small head. The boy strode to and fro, stretching a thin line from the cage on the stand to the house. His hair was mussed, standing erect, vital, his young overgrown body quick and sure. Then he was finished. They tested it. He raised his ruddy hand in signal.

Her trembling finger came to the button. The door sprang down with a faint clash.

Over two days she waited, leashing her patience. She had baited the trap with pieces of fruit and crumbs of cake. The bare blackened arms of the giant cherry trees spread angrily behind the yard where the snow was melting, making black pools. The network of twigs seemed to quiver in sympathy with her concentration. She did not sleep deeply at night and her limbs ached through the day from turning and moving in the bed with vague dreams.

That first evening the gray bird had come straight to the cage, hung in the tiny doorway and pecked at the bait within, making the trap his own. She tightened her fists, but she was hopeful. He perched on the wire roof and spread his matchstick legs. And when the little redbird flew foolish down into the pear tree, he made it scurry, a red disappearing fragment. The wind blew his feathers, puffing saucy.

In the muffled light of next morning she lay still under her blankets, trying to remember. Why did her thin blood beat in this erratic way? Why was she disturbed? It came to her. This could be the day! She thrust the warmth away and poked her feet into the felt slippers. She scurried to the window. What was that in the cage? In the murky light it was difficult to be sure. Her old black eyes peered; her forehead pressed on the pane. Yes, something moved. Her finger went to the button and touched it.

The little clashing noise. Incredible! The whirling desperate flutter. The tiny cyclone of gray feathers. And then the bird was still. Was it frightened? She got the mackinaw he had used to wear, from the clothes-tree, and pulled on her boots. Her robe trailed in the wet grass as she stepped out in the early light. The snow was completely gone; it was warm, like spring. A patch of red burned in the east where clouds were standing back for the sun. The tall trees were observing her, holding their breath.

With guilty crouch, she came up to the cage. The bird battered its wings suddenly, rattling the wire. She grasped the handle and stumbled to the house down the cellar-stairs. She set it on a dusty bench in the dark, and climbed back up the stairs very slowly now. But each foot planted was a song of joy. "The daemon! I've got him now."

She had to go back to bed, weakly drawing up the covers. As she had passed the window, she had seen one or two already hopping in the rosy air. The horizon was a band of pink and yellow and orange. She waited for her pulse to slow, making her mind a blank. "I'll think about it later."

It had begun to seep into her consciousness. "What will I do with him?" Could she have him transported and released somewhere? There must be a law against trapping a songbird. How brutal it sounded. But no matter how far he was taken, he would return. She knew it. Birds could fly incredible distances. He would come back, unerring. She skirmished about the point, finally facing it. Murder. Could she murder? For the sake of the others. She put it from her willfully. And then had to take it up again. She would murder him. But after a while.

And then all her birds had come back. It was as if there had been no gray intruder. Even a squirrel was loping merrily across the yard, up the pear trunk, leaping over to the feed stand, sitting up like a little bear, holding a crust in its paws. The sun flung forth in yellow sweetness, making the winter day lovely. And down in the dark cellar he was, soundless.

Slowly, compelled, she descended. Motionless, he stared at her. When she made a movement, there was a spinning of gray and white and a feather fell on the cement floor. Then he waited, one black eye flashing in the dim light. "I must do it," she said strongly, as if she were a young girl and fearless, and it were a thing to do.

She hunted out a heavy rag from a sack that hung in a musty corner. She slid up the cage-door while he cowered. Her bony hand went in and he cried, squeaking then so the sound seared her mind. Her fingers plucked the delicate twig-like legs, felt the biting sharp bill, and he lay soft and hot, helpless, in her palm. Quickly she covered him with the little rug. Her heart bounded frightened, and bounded again. There was a dark taste in the back of her mouth; she began to tremble violently. "I cannot do it. I must." She took a hammer and beat the stuffed rag repeatedly, pounding at the lump in it. "He is dead." It was instant. He made no noise. "He never knew!"

The blood was rushing in her throat and she dragged herself to the bottom step, dropping the hammer, holding the bundle weakly. "I wish I hadn't done it now." Her limbs shook, and she forced herself to reel in the faintness that came over her; hand over hand, she hauled it in. The bundle was now at her feet. The crushed brightness. The bold song. But he had been too cruel, this daemon. There had been no other way. This one bird. One time.

"Is it all right," she pleaded, "that I did it? What do you say? You always understood?" She sat alone.

After a while she stirred and nodded. She cradled the wrapped rag and labored up the steps from the darkness to the bright outdoors. She put it in the trash can among the litter. "No use thinking on it. It's done." And when the paper boy came, she told him to take back the wired gadget. "I decided against using it," she lied. "You don't mind?" She couldn't let a child know of her deed.

"That's all right, missus. That's the fun of it." He was cheery. He got the trap and put it under his arm. "It was keen anyhow, rigging it."

She took up the old pattern of her days. No evil plummeted from the rooftop. There was serenity and order in the back clearing. Winter passed and spring had come. She would sit in the window sewing or sipping a cup of tea to warm her slow-moving blood. Morning and night she'd rise to go with the feed pan onto the young greening lawn, putting out tidbits. One time twin snow-white birds came. She wrote it in her log-book and underscored it: *Two city pigeons today*. The next evening,

---

The Daemon

a blue-gray one landed with them, flapping, her neck irides-
cent, gold and red in the sun.

The leaves unfolded in the new season, the trees taking on a
misty sea-color. Suddenly, it was summer. The foliage was full
blown and the noonday hot. The heavy branches joined in a
green circle about her back yard, forming a bower, a bright
scene.

She was happy. She'd dragged the wicker chair onto the lawn
near the two stands and in the cool hours would sit out there. A
few flowers had sprung wayward from old seed, for she was too
weary to make a garden this year. They sprinkled color in the
corners, a red one, a pink, a bed of lacy white ones. She'd lean
back in her chair, and sparrows and sometimes the redbird came
to perch on its wicker back, without fear. She smiled softly.
When she brought peanuts and put them out, it was no time at
all before the squirrels found them. She had to laugh at three of
them, springing across the yard, sitting up to split the nuts,
ignoring the jays who arrived in a gay crowd, screaming like
bells. There were great black crows too, sometimes. Solemn
they strolled, dwarfing the other birds, before flapping ponder-
ously away.

The darkness would come down gently, and just before it laid
its dusky blanket, the emerald grass would gleam one last time,
the heady rose color of sunset would blaze, the great trees
would tower like a tender collective clan of mothers. And the
last bird would wing silent to where it spent its night. She
would sigh and force her limbs forward, rise and take her way to
the house. She would have a slice of toast and a buttered egg
and her cup of sweetened tea. And then to bed. Summer played
its days out like a careless child throwing stones in a bottomless
pond. Too soon it was so chill that she couldn't stay outdoors.
The wind howled down from the north and clouds hovered,
sagging with snow. Her bones hurt sometimes, strange twinges
suddenly catching her. She missed the heat of the sun. One
afternoon as she sat in the window, she noticed no birds at the

stands. "There must be a dog about," she muttered, searching to see if one had passed. But there was nothing. Then a gray swift form flew into the pear tree.

The next day it was the same, one or two birds lingering in the outlying winter-stripped trees, but none daring to come closer. She took her dish of feed out. The black eye of the mockingbird fixed on her, as he perched in the pear tree. He was rounder, fluffier than the one of the previous year. She grasped the branch suddenly to shake it. He held on, his spread wings balancing him. "You again! Daemon!" She hurled the dish, the grain spilling. Then he was winging, and out of sight.

When she had hung her coat and come to the window, her dry lips were set. She saw a few return. "It's no use," she said. "He'll be back."

By afternoon, the yard was deserted. When the doorbell rang, she had to force the strength to rise and answer it. Her eyes had dulled and she scarcely recognized the paper boy. He came in to wait while she found the change to pay him.

"You know, I was thinking about that trap I set up for you last year, missus," he said.

"What?"

"You've forgot about it, but I had a fine time. Often wondered why you wouldn't use it. Too soft, I guess, you were?"

"I could never do it again. You go now."

"Goodbye, missus."

She stood in the hall a while after he'd gone, and shivered in the stale empty air. There was no heart in her for the effort it would take to make tea. She eased her bones into the chair overlooking the back view. In the gray half-light, the great trees were silhouetted against a violent brooding sky. Grasping, they twined upward, twisted. The daemon-form was in the tree, preening his wings with a knifelike bill. Now he was gone, coursing after one of her fleeing pets. In the distance crows barked, and the gray bird came to squat again in the low pear limb. She rocked, alone, waiting.

The Daemon

The Black and the White Rabbit

Ever since they married and she moved up a flight to the larger apartment, Margret had sworn that the cat would come back and find her. And there Kat was one windy January day when she returned from shopping. "Just look who's here, Warren!" She met him at the door, jubilant.

"Remarkable." He kissed the end of Margret's snub nose.

"She's that way too. In a condition."

"How nice. What I can't see is why she runs away from you in the first place."

"Kat's independent. She doesn't need anybody. And she always comes back." The animal was delicate-featured, with fawn coat and sleek black tail and face and paws. Margret, holding her, looked like a little girl, in brown slacks, white shirt, a yellow sweater flung on her shoulders. Her face was oval and eyes blue-white. Warren thought, you can't look deep into them, for they reflect like mirrors. He saw his two selves in the black pupils, tall-bodied, close-cropped graying hair, big pipe in teeth, a red-striped final copy of the *Star* under his arm. He couldn't notice the honey-dark color of his skin.

Warren's wife was Swedish, and they'd seen each other a year before deciding to marry. When he'd told his mother, Susanne, of their plans, she'd merely stood up from her place at the supper table like some actress playing tragedy, and declared,

"Go ahead! You will; you're obstinate. But I don't wish to meet the girl. Don't bring her here."

"Susanne, don't be unkind. She's alone in America."

But Susanne turned her back on him and went to her piano. Before she touched the keys she looked across the room. "Trouble. You'll see."

He was angry. "You hunt for it, Susanne. There are a million kinds of trouble; you lump them all into that one."

Susanne began to play. She was fragile and light-skinned for her race, and rather haughty. She worked in the Music Division of the Library of Congress. When Warren was a boy, growing up in Washington, she'd do something that seemed cruel to him later, but it was like his mother. She'd put him before a mirror. "Now look at yourself good, Warren. You're colored. You've got just enough tone in your skin so it can't be mistaken. Whenever you get mixed up about it, you go and look in a glass."

"Yes, ma'am." But he hadn't been interested. He'd simply planned on staying out of the South; let it simmer behind its iron curtain, he thought. Maybe he wasn't a fighting kind of man. All he wanted was a quiet home and a quiet life. Susanne said his father was that way too; somebody really had to poke him before he'd take offense. He'd died of some illness when Warren was three, and he didn't remember him at all. Susanne never remarried; she said there'd been only one made like him.

Warren enjoyed his job, and he enjoyed acting too. There was an amateur dramatic club at State, where he worked in Educational Exchange. He was in practically every production they put on. He'd met Margret at that club. She'd just joined and was delegated to play the piano between the acts of "The Face on the Bar Room Floor." She could sing too in a reedy voice that went well with his baritone.

So there she stood with Kat in her arms. "Wherever will we put her kittens!"

The Black and the White Rabbit

"The laundry basket?"

"Good idea. Wonder where she's been? She only has one little scratch, Warren."

"Did you go to see Dr. Cooper today?"

"Um hum."

He went into their tiny kitchen and got some ice and poured a little bourbon in a glass. He ran some Potomac sludge from the tap into it and saluted the two of them in the doorway. "Welcome home, little cat."

"Thanks," Margret said. Then she looked a little lost suddenly. "Dr. Cooper says it's true about me."

He set his drink on the icebox quickly. His throat closed. He'd always thought he didn't want a child, until Margret told him that moment. He tried to say it to her, and she put the cat on the floor and came to him.

Late that night, in their one comfortable large chair, Margret was in her favorite place, his lap. He stroked her yellow hair, leaning her head back onto his shoulder. The old record player was repeating one side over and over. They liked folksongs. Margret tried hard to seem a native of the country; it had been six years since she left Sweden. She began singing alone, subduing her funny accent. Kat was on the braided rug near the bedroom door, licking her sides. A sensation of peace grew up slowly in the warm room like some kind of flower. There was a child crying off in another part of the thin-walled apartment house. Warren wondered what sorrow or unfinished need made it wail so steadily. In the flat above them, a man began to cough in a lengthy spasm. The first night they moved in, Warren had heard the sound. Car lights had flashed along the wallpaper from the hot summer street below. Margret's breathing had been even and deep; she was tired out from the moving. The hollow gasp had continued and he'd felt an unease. He'd grown accustomed to it, and his wife never appeared to notice.

She laid her hand on his cheek and patted it. He continued to stroke her hair, listening to Burl Ives telling about the black-haired girl and to Margret's accompanying voice. The child stopped crying. Kat rose and meowed and stretched. Warren thought, three of us; an oval-faced son of mine. My mother'll stop her foolishness and come to visit us then. Susanne will be a grandmother. I'll buy her the children's book about the white and the black rabbit who had a very nice time together.

Three months went by serenely. Margret stayed well; she lighted her husband's pipe in the evenings, played with Kat's three lively kittens that lived in the laundry basket, kept the two-rooms-and-a-kitchen tidy, and cooked tolerably. They made plans for the coming baby, decided to invest in a piano for Margret, and talked about Warren's two-week leave which they'd spend in New York with friends of his in the Village. He wanted to show them his beautiful fruitful wife.

Then a thing of great moment came along. Margret became ill and nearly lost her baby. In March she'd had a slight cold that persisted. Now she lay abed and Dr. Cooper said must remain there until September if she was to carry the child to completion. Five long months! Her blue-white frightened eyes flung back his image and she withdrew. She denied his efforts to comfort her.

"But the doctor says there's no danger as long as you're good!"

"I'm all alone," she said angrily, "and I'm afraid."

"I'm here."

"Not all day long."

"But you've always been alone then, Margret."

"I went shopping, and to the Library."

"I'll bring you books. And you have Kat."

"Your mother should come and talk with me. She could spare the time. It's her son's child. Never would a mother-in-law do that in Sverige."

"I'm sorry. Susanne's stubborn."

"She dislikes me, Warren. And she's never even met me."

"I'll ask her again."

"I don't want her now." Margaret's face got sullen, her eyes
over-bright. She scratched behind Kat's ears softly. "I have my
cat."

He found homes for the three kittens; they were too much
for Warren with the flat to straighten now, and the cooking to
do. He hired a girl to come on Wednesdays to clean and wash
and iron, but he had to save their money which was disappearing rapidly. At night he stretched out like a long cold stone
beside his poor wife. When she complained that her eyes hurt,
he read aloud, sometimes past midnight. Then he would fall
asleep with sad thoughts uppermost. He dreamed of unpleasant
occurrences and woke in the night, sometimes to find her weeping. He took her and held her small slightly swollen frame in his
arms that were of little help now.

Songs came up from the street. It may have seemed that
Warren wasn't proud of being black. That wasn't so. It simply
wasn't an earth-shaking attribute to him; it never seemed of
great significance. Not more interesting than his wife being
Swedish and therefore having certain Scandinavian ethnic
traits. Margret would laugh at the Swedes, saying they were
natural pessimists, due to their lives being made of short lovely
summers and dreary interminable winters. Warren told her he
would be the optimist and quoted the old joke: If you could
become a black man for a Saturday night, you'd never wish to
be white again.

Their neighborhood was mixed; there were Italians, Poles,
Negroes, and a scattering of Chinese, Syrians, Indians, and for-
eign-speaking Europeans. In the evenings, the young Negroes
sang as they passed. Maybe they liked to identify with the
darkness. Like Hughes' lines, *Night coming tenderly Black like
me.* Sometimes they were combos, and good enough for dive
work or even better-class clubs:

> *Diamond Jim's a gambler,*
> *He must be satan sent,*
> *He'd rather be a gambler*

Than the Vice President!
Man, oh man!

The white man didn't give out like that where you could hear him. Not in Washington, D.C. Warren didn't know why.

Lately Susanne had been on his mind. She wouldn't think much of Margret's sulking about her misfortune, he thought. His mother had a brash outlook when it came to pity. He phoned her once in a while, but it was plain to him while they talked that she was determined to stay clear of them.

Then a letter arrived from overseas. Margret's mother would be landing in the country in a few days for a visit with her daughter and her new son-in-law. Warren thought Margret might have let him in on it that she'd been invited, but he held his tongue. Fru Berg arrived a day earlier than expected. The girl had come in and left a bucket of sootish water in the middle of the room, a dust mop by the bed. Warren had taken the afternoon off and was washing the windows inside and out on a stepladder, wearing old torn jeans and a ragged shirt. A fine spring wind had risen and the Bach choral mass was on the record machine, its heavy tones surging about so no one could talk.

There was the woman in the doorway, a bird-cage clutched in one black-gloved hand. "Dotter!" Her heavy voice came over the music. "Hur står det till?"

Warren leapt off his perch and caught the arm of the record player so it skimmed whining, scratching.

Margret went white. "I'm okay, mor."

"Why are you in the bed then," she growled. Her pale eyes swept over Warren. "You're the husband?"

"Sure." He spread wet hands, laughing and shrugging. "Can't shake, but welcome anyway."

"Tack." Her freckled face was self-possessed. Under the lilac-flowered hat, her hair was auburn. She was short and broad-hipped and wore a purple suit. She set the cage down by the door and the bird fluttered about in it. Kat came down off the bed in a slinky stride.

Margret patted the covers and smiled. "Mor, how I've longed to see you. Take off your hat. How is everyone at home?"

Warren took the pail and rags and left them. "I'll make a pot of tea, Margret."

"Okay. Thanks." She was sounding gay again.

There came the rise and fall of their talking from the other room, while he waited for the water to boil and sent the girl out for a chicken for supper. Then there was a cry from Margret and a shocked silence. Warren ran in. Kat had murdered the bird, her long paws thrust through the bars.

"Such a dreadful creature, now!" Fru Berg plucked off her hat and flung it at the cat, who scrambled yowling out into the kitchen.

Margret began to cry. "No she's not. Oh, Kat!"

"Come along, fru Berg," Warren said. "We'll have some tea while your daughter rests."

She consented and after they'd shut the door, he explained Margret's illness. "She'll be all right now you're here. A little visiting is all she needs. She's lonely, that's it." He poured the tea and hoped the old woman didn't look too closely at their quarters, which seemed suddenly shabby to him, looking at them with her close eye.

As if there hadn't been enough going on, when the chicken was brought in, Kat scuttled past the girl's legs into the corridor and that was that. The animal never could bear a stranger near her mistress, and only by a noble effort had resigned herself to Warren. He'd grown attached to her, and before two days were out, began to miss Kat's raucous conversational calling. Warren mentioned it to Margret, who was dry-eyed. "This time she's left me for good, Warren. I feel it." Margret spoke as if she'd barred her pet from her mind.

Supper was over, and Warren was trying to feel at ease, sitting on the bed by his wife. "No. She always comes back."

Children and Lovers

Fru Berg sat in the rocker across the room. "I'll buy you a new cat, dotter."

Warren stroked Margret's hair. "She wants this one."

The man upstairs began coughing in one of his prolonged spells. Margret waited until he had finished, her brows knit. "Every night since we moved into this flat he's done that. I think he's dying."

"Margret," Warren said, "stop."

"I'm sorry, Warren."

Fru Berg rocked vigorously, pushing the needle through the little cloth she'd taken from her bag. Warren got up and walked about the room, hampered by the short space for his long legs and heavy body. He felt the female eyes following him, the hostile, alien, white-skinned womenkind. How strange the two of them seemed suddenly to him.

After the mother-in-law had been there a few weeks, Warren went to visit Susanne one evening before going home from the office. She was in the same apartment, quiet and roomy. "I thought you'd be getting a smaller place, Susanne, when I moved out."

"I like it here," his mother laughed.

He sat down to rest, thinking he found little peace at home nowadays. The old woman rocked and sewed beside Margret all the time. In the mornings Warren had to tiptoe through the living room where she slept on the sofa, her belongings scattered about. He breakfasted in the snack bar at State. Susanne had no use for his problem. "What'll I do?"

"Send Mama packing."

"Margret likes the company. I shouldn't complain."

"They're playing a game of *grandes dames* with you."

"Susanne, don't be like that."

But she would do no more than give him a plate of crackers and cheese and a glass of red wine to warm his stomach for the streetcar trip home. There his son lay hidden within his wife, he thought, unnoticed between the two women; his skin must be honey dark and soft, his blue eyes sad like Margret's. When Warren reached the flat, fru Berg had made a proposition. Margret was flushed with excitement, leaning forward from her white pillows.

"Mor must take the boat next week. She's offered to pay passage for me to go with her, Warren."

"Margrét! It's only three months more. The doctor—"

"We called Dr. Cooper and he says I may if I don't lift a finger and lie in the cabin all the trip."

"You've wasted no time!"

"I want to go home."

"This is home."

"No!" She refused it, her eyes on fire.

"But you're doing so well. What do you want? My promise that you'll have no more children?"

"It's not that, Warren."

He looked at fru Berg. "Don't take her away from me."

"I'm thinking of her, young man."

Margret took Warren's hand. "You could stay with your mother until I come back."

"You won't be back. I know it. You're running away from me."

For the first time in how long, she was smiling lovingly, relieved. "Of course I will!"

The bitter anger lay dry on the back of Warren's tongue. Some boys were walking below on the spring-swept-cement, clapping their hands to the rhythm:

> *Fee Fi Fo Fum!*
> *True love, don't weep, here I come.*
>
> (Clap clap)
>
> *Some day someone's gonna see*
> *The green grass growing over me!*
>
> (Clap clap clap clap)

Children and Lovers

"Warren, aren't you listening to me?" fru Berg asked.

"What did you say?"

"You can come too. You'll find work there."

Margret was pleased. "I didn't think of that. We have enough in the bank, I'm sure."

"This is my land, fru Berg." His firm loud statement surprised even Warren. "The land of my fathers and of my children."

"In Sverige you'd find no grudge against your race," she offered in a wheedling way. "We don't think of things like that."

"She's right," Margret said.

The mother-in-law continued. "You must consider Margret's baby. Do you want the child to carry your people's load on his back? Don't you think about him?"

That struck home. But Warren said softly, "He's in my thoughts all the time." He turned to his wife, who was sitting up in the bed now, alert. "In this land his roots are fast. They go back to the first slave and the first master. His fathers have made a place where he belongs. You understand, don't you? That this is his homeland we're giving him."

She avoided his eyes. "I don't know what to do any longer, Warren."

"You used to know!"

"Remember," fru Berg put in hastily, "the baby's half svenska."

Warren addressed her quietly and coldly. "Let Margret speak." He watched his wife intently. "You've changed. All your will is gone."

"I promise to come back," she cried.

"When?"

"I don't know. I promise though!"

Warren determined to make the best of it, when he saw how Margret would not be turned. He went about his work conscious of the blow soon to fall. The week was over, the last day

---

The Black and the White Rabbit

had come. As the hour for leaving the flat approached, Margret became nervous, sitting in the big easy chair, rubbing her white gloves together, tapping the soles of her low-heeled white shoes. Fru Berg was still in the bedroom. "Feel all right?" Warren asked.

"Maybe it isn't good after all, Warren." Margret frowned.

"What do you mean?"

"I feel there's something I haven't done, something that needs attending."

"Change your mind; don't go. That's what it is."

"Please, Warren. Let me think."

He looked at the clock. "It's time."

"All right."

He got the bags and fru Berg settled her hat. The women preceded Warren into the hall. As he was going through the door, the phone rang. "One minute. I'll get it," he told them, setting the bags down.

It was Susanne. "I suppose it's foolish to call at the eleventh hour. You'll be putting them on their way soon."

"Susanne! I am now."

"I thought next week."

"Now. This minute."

"Well, let me say it. I've been thinking, stubborn as you are, you'll never have the sense to give up that white girl. So tell her if she wants to stay, I'd come over Sunday and cook supper. Matter of fact, I have some steaks in the freezer here. I'll bring them along."

"You're crazy," Warren cried. "You could have offered before. They're clutching their tickets!"

There was a pause. "She's probably had enough of your life anyway."

Warren pursed his mouth. "You play only one tune, don't you? No, truly Margret's sick. She's going just to be with her mother."

"Is that the twist? A Mama girl?"

"I don't know any longer. I can't think."

The door to the flat banged loudly, and Warren looked up. Margret had entered the room, her eyes wild. Against her breast she clasped the loudly purring Kat, coat bedraggled, long claws firmly fixed in the lace of Margret's summer dress. "Look! She was sitting in the hall!"

He rose up, the phone hanging from his hand. "Welcome home, Kat."

"Whatever shall I do, Warren? Tell me!"

"She seems to be in a condition too." Warren shook his head, clucking.

"But I can't just leave her."

Susanne's voice whined through the ear-piece. "Are you there? You haven't answered me."

"I can't, when she's come back again. Can I, Warren?" Margret was sinking into the large chair. "Oh, how comfortable this is. She must have been the unfinished thing I was worrying about. Don't you see?"

Fru Berg bustled through the doorway, waving her black purse wrathfully. "We're late! Hurry." She stopped before her daughter. "Margret, whatever are you doing holding that creature? She's tearing your dress."

"No she's not, mor," Margret said happily. "Kat's too clever."

Warren lifted the phone to his ear. Susanne was demanding, "I want to speak with Margret. Is she there yet? Put her on."

"Yes, she's here. And my son. Also Kat."

Warren gave the phone to his wife. He looked across the room into the mirror, straightening his tie, feeling that the end had become the beginning as so often happens.

The Black and the White Rabbit

The Goose

"No," Bengt said at noon as the snow stopped falling.

"But I want to go."

"I'll take you next week." Powerful, her husband strode past her, out of the kitchen, back to the cornfield.

Bengt and the hired man were getting in the last of the crop. The fall wind came whirling at Elsa standing in the entry where the snow melted into pools on the floor, watching Bengt go, pulling her sweater about her. She wanted to visit Grandpop tomorrow, not next week. He was getting old and had never seen his great-grandchildren, Bo and Tina. And tomorrow was his eightieth birthday! Ever since Grandmom had passed away a dozen years ago, he'd lived alone in a country town a hundred miles to the south in Wisconsin, in a small white house that was slowly falling down.

Elsa heard the faraway goose gabble and shielded her eyes. The sun blazed, a flower in a clear blue field. Their farm was on one of the great Canada Goose highways, and when the migrations were in full swing sometimes the sky would be full of them, in long lines, forming v's and again single-file, serpent-like, wavering across the sky.

"Kwonk, onk! Honk!" She could hear their wings fanning as they passed close overhead, long necks stretched out. She listened for the popping sound that would be hunters but there was nothing.

186

Then over the goose sound came a slow wail from Bo as he woke in his cot and she turned. His nap was over. Bo was past three but Elsa, indulgent in the way of country women, still gave him a bottle sometimes. He'd nearly given it up for a cup when he was eighteen months old and Tina arrived.

Now Elsa filled a bottle with the milk she'd got that morning from the goats that lived in a shed behind the big Holstein cowbarn, not far from where Elsa's hens were kept. She fitted the nipple and took it in. Bo's small roar ceased and his eyes gazed at her, blue and wide, as she helped him pull on his corduroy pants and his sweater. He scrambled to his feet, the bottle in one hand and followed her to the baby's room, curly-haired, blond, big for his age.

Tina was awake, waiting. Gentle, a blue-eyed Swede like all the family, she lay with her covers cast back, her toes in her fingers, content. Bo leaned on a chair arm, his milk in one hand, a leg crossed, serious.

"You remember Grandpop?" Elsa asked him.

"Grandpop," Bo said, and she knew he'd forgot. He'd seen the old man, Elsa's grandfather, once. That was when her parents had died in an accident two years ago and Bengt had driven over to Grandpop's town and brought him to the funeral. Bo had been a year old.

Grandpop had disapproved of the marriage of Elsa's parents, and so Elsa had seen little of him in her childhood. She hardly knew him. He had a white beard and pale blue eyes and stood stern and straight-backed, offering the child Elsa candy from a slim glass jar he took from the sideboard.

Grandpop was seventy-nine now, and insisted upon living alone, batching in the house where he and Grandmom had always lived, where he still burned coal-oil lamps, refusing electricity or telephones. When Grandmom died, Elsa had tried to coax him to come live with them. But he refused to be transplanted. Though he'd spent his life in a constant verbal disagreement with Grandmom, they had been inseparable.

Bo sucked at the emptied bottle for a moment, took it from his mouth, sighed, let it fall with a thud on the rag-woven rug. Like a baby viking, he strode from her into his world of a wagon and wooden horses he dragged through the low-ceilinged farmhouse.

Elsa picked up Tina, soft and chubby, clutching her bottle. She sat in the rocker. She felt a loneliness now and then for her own mother and Tina helped fill the void. Tina or Bo or Bengt. And perhaps Grandpop too. While he was yet alive. Maybe he had need of her as much as she him; he had no one. After her parents' funeral, as fierce as when Grandmom had died, he'd rejected Elsa and Bengt's offer to come live with them.

On a dark wall of the living room were snapshots, one of Grandpop and one of Grandmom too. Grandpop wore suspenders over his frail stiff shoulders and held a spread black umbrella to ward off the sun, standing guardian over his flower garden. He always counted blooms. "Today," he had used to tell Grandmom while the child Elsa listened, "seventeen daisies, twelve roses, and three of those new-fangled kind of larkspur." His lilac bush reached over the second-storey windows! The photo of Grandmom showed a large gaunt-faced woman on the back porch of the little house, holding an oven-fresh pie out to the photographer.

Tina finished her milk and Elsa took her to the kitchen. She set her on a rug in the corner and penned her in with three chairs turned on their sides. Tina had learned to crawl and got into everything. Elsa pounded down her bread dough and kneaded it on the floured table. She formed the loaves and set them to rise while she fired the stove afresh to heat the oven. Then she broke eggs and stirred up a white cake. She made a custard filling with the yolks, bright orange from the new corn she was feeding the hens.

By four it was nearly time for the fall dusk to descend in its usual hurry. Elsa was topping the cake in white sugary swirls. The kitchen was fragrant with the odor of baking bread, and

Elsa turned to take the loaves out. The wandering geese called again outside. Even Bo listened, lifting his head and pointing up, letting his horses be.

"Mama. Bird."

"Geese."

"Geese?"

Elsa took his hand and they went outside the door to watch. They stood on the porch, the child like the mother hugging his arms, warm-blooded Scandinavians in the cold air. It was the hour when the birds were seeking landing places for the night, preferring lake or swamp. Sometimes they traveled a thousand miles a day, it was said, and though they were fat and heavy-breasted when the journey began, they needed to eat along the way. They were huge fowl, sometimes over three feet long from beak to tail-tip, and weighing near fifteen pounds. They wanted to land now in their sloping drifting way, to settle on water with a splash, to feed there on eelgrasses, sedges, insects, small fish. Or to come down in farmers' stubble grain fields. Bengt welcomed them on his farm. He loved the geese and never begrudged their meal as some did. And Bengt permitted no hunters, either.

But there were always men with long-barreled guns on the bordering farms, who knew the ancient paths of the winged migrants. Elsa heard the shots.

"Bang, bang," said Bo.

She watched the flock overhead. One goose staggered in the sky on one wing, riding a wind tide and failing. Elsa walked alarmed, away from Bo, down the snow-cleared steps into the yard. She watched the bird as it drifted, flapping, into the wood half a mile away.

She hurried back into the kitchen, shooing Bo before her. She caught Tina up and put her in her high-barred bed. The baby, docile, her thumb in her mouth, didn't mind. Elsa helped Bo slip into his sweater, which she'd knit, blue and red striped, thick-wooled, high-necked. She set him to tugging on his knee-boots. And she got into her old galoshes, the ones she wore when tending her hens and going about the goats in their stable. She wore a long brown wrap and a dark shawl shrouding her form.

"Hurry, it's getting dark," she urged Bo.

Against the porch wall stood a little toboggan Bengt had made last year, with a slatted back rest and sides, so her babies couldn't fall out. She set it flat and Bo climbed into it. "Goose?" he asked.

"Hurry," she whispered. And she was running down the road to the woods, pulling the sled by its rope, Bo squealing with pleasure.

But the snow-clothed woods were huge and shadowy, and the bird was nowhere to be seen. She wandered up and down the paths and through the bush, dragging Bo behind, making new marks on the untracked white. Then when the twilight was just at hand she saw it, stone-still by a tree, a button eye fixed on her. The great bird's head and neck were black, a white band ran from eye to eye under the head; its back and wings were mantled gray-brown and its breast was almost white.

Elsa glanced back at Bo and put her fingers to her lips. "Shhhh."

But Bo shouted, "Bird!"

"Stay there, silly," she told him as the goose ran from her on its strong web-feet.

It flapped, dragging the wounded wing, gasping, hissing. "Quonk!"

Elsa panted after it, slipping in the fresh-fallen snow as they rounded trees and bushes. The goose scuttled into a brush of young aspen and Elsa plunged upon it, on her knees. She clasped its wings fast to its sides, lifted it in her arms, the red staining her dark shawl. "There now."

It ceased to struggle, breathing open-beaked, its black eyes terrified. She carried it, heavy and warm against her, back to Bo, who sat solemn on his sled, blue eyes wide and worried, his mittened hands under him to warm them.

With the goose under an arm, she pulled the toboggan back up the road, going in the old tracks she'd made before. The dark came falling down, and by the time they reached the goat shed she was stumbling on the unclear path.

Bo scrambled from his sled and followed her in. Elsa put the bird down in the corn-shuck fodder in a corner pen. From a high peg she took the coal-oil lantern and scratched the heavy match. The light wavered. The five milking does and the two fall-born kids were crowding at the pen lattice, pushing each other, shoving Bo, who leaned on the gate to look.

Elsa set out a pan of water and shelled corn before the new-comer. She remembered old tales told. Her farmer father had said a wild goose would settle down with a domestic flock and even pair off and raise young. It would seem content over a winter, staying sometimes two or three years. Then one day when a wild flock came screaming over, up it would rush and be gone for good, the strong old blood owning it.

"Eat, goose." Bo beat on the gate with his mittens.

Elsa shelled corn for the goats in their wood trough. She pulled hay down for them. She told Bo, "Give him time."

The white-bearded man with the candy jar had told another kind of tale to the child Elsa, of seven white geese in a Swedish forest who were seven brothers and it took a kiss or some act of goodness, of charity, to free the bewitched.

The wild bird stood hostile; Elsa felt its pain. The one wing drooped, the near-white feather edges pink-tinged. It didn't even turn its bill to preen itself; it would not glance at the feed before it. With eyes dark and moist it followed Elsa's movements, unmoving; it was a changling prince. Elsa thought how before it was too late, Bo ought to know of Grandpop's stories too.

"Eat, bird!" Bo shouted.

"You'll see your grandpop tomorrow," Elsa said, swinging the lantern before Bo as they went to the house. "You're old enough to understand some of his tales."

And that was what she declared to Bengt at the supper table. "Sure," he said, "and I'll take you down to visit as soon as the corn's in, wife. We're in the middle of it."

"But not till next week!"

"What's the big hurry?"

"It's his birthday!"

"And it's a hundred miles to go," Bengt growled. "You think you can manage Bo and Tina and drive too. That old Chevy's a rattletrap."

"Bird!" Bo shouted at them, untouched by their combat.

"Goose," Elsa sighed. "Say goose, silly."

"Goose, Papa." Bo's blue eyes were pale with his elation.

Bengt told Bo, "I saw a goose shot down over a lake when I was your size. Dove right down under and stayed with only the beak above water."

"Hurt?" Bo asked, half-comprehending.

"Hunter had got it. But your papa stayed in the brush and watched. When they went away, the goose came up on land and grazed a while and then took off."

Bo gazed up at him. "Bird won't eat, Papa."

"Will you look in on it while we're away?" Elsa asked.

Bengt flushed darkly. "Haven't I made myself clear, wife!"

She stood up and began to clear the table, her mouth set. A tall woman, strong despite her slender body, she wore her heavy blond hair twisted in a rope about her head. She was as stubborn a Swede as her husband, she thought. "And tend the goats and my hens," she coaxed. "And I'll stay one night away only. I've baked bread ahead for you." She leaned over her husband in his chair, her breasts on his shoulders, her cheek on his hair.

"I'm taking Grandpop two loaves. And I made him a white cake."

Children and Lovers

Bengt pushed her from him, rising. "Seems I'm no master in my own house!" He stalked from the room, getting his pipe, clattering about, his movements heavy and strong.

He heard her in the kitchen, teaching Bo a riddle. "What goes to bed with its shoes on?"

"A horse," Bo said. "But why, Mama?" He tried to understand.

"Not Bo!" Elsa teased, leading him to his cot, passing Tina, who was long since asleep. "Bo takes off his boots. And Grandpop too!"

"Grandpop," said Bo. "Who's Grandpop?"

"Tomorrow," she promised. "And he's your great-grandpop, too."

In the cold dawn Bengt watched them go down the snow-rutted road. Elsa, waving back, thought he looked lonely and for a moment she doubted her stubborn decision. Why couldn't the birthday wait a week? The old lumbering Chevy sedan was cold; the wind leaked in through the rattling windows. She had a blanket over her knees and one over Bo's. Tina was in the big washbasket on the floor in back, Elsa's pillow for a mattress and a wool rug over her. Tina had on a striped knit sweater too, from the same yarn skeins as Bo's, red and blue, and a bottle was tucked beside her. Bo crawled in back, dragging his blanket, and fell asleep on the seat. Elsa hummed to herself.

The trip took half a day. Bo and Elsa were munching on slabs of her bread put together with butter, as they came into the town where Grandpop lived. Tina was awake, crumbs of bread in her fingers too. They braked before the small tumbling-down house, behind the rickety picket fence and the winter-bare snowball shrubs and the high-branched lilac of the front yard. Elsa saw the half-dozen bottles of milk outside on the porch, the frozen cream risen into a tall cylinder on each, topped with the paper cap. And the snow-smooth walkway, untouched by boots.

The Goose

She frowned, leaning back to lift Tina in her arms, hurrying up the walk. Bo scrambled behind. She knocked and no one came. She waited and knocked again. The knob turned easily and Elsa went in, down the hallway, the old house scent familiar to her, made of life-long arguments and old sheets and blankets, of oven-fresh pies and jars of just-picked iris and larkspur, of fairy tales and unquenched fatherly anger. Elsa's boots were quick down the hall, her voice anxious.

"Grandpop?"

The house was cold and silent. She ran through the living room, the kitchen. She found him in the bedroom, propped on pillows, the bed shoved to the window, the rug disarrayed. Blankets were heaped on him; a soup bowl, crusted, was on the bedside table.

At first she thought he was gone, but his eyes opened, pale and faraway. "Who are you? What do you want?"

"Is there coal in the cellar, Grandpop?"

He shut his eyes weakly on her. Hastily she set Tina on the floor. "You watch her," she told Bo. But Tina began to wail, sensing the strangeness, the desertion. Even Bo's mouth turned down. So Elsa took them to the living room and shut them in there. "Take care of Tina, silly," she said, and the baby's cry followed her to the cellar. She knew Bo was making up his mind whether or not to roar too.

Elsa started a fire with kindling in the furnace, and when it caught, she heaped on coal she shoveled from the pile in the corner. She hurried back up. Bo sat by his sister, a proprietary hand on her woolly figure.

"Good Bo." Elsa went in to Grandpop.

"Are you Elsa?" he said.

"Why didn't you send for me!"

"Figured when the man came with next week's milk, he'd see me from the window."

"Grandpop."

"Wanted to reach eighty and I made it. I'm ready to go. That's a good age. My grandfather fought against Napoleon and he came home to Marstrand and lived to be eighty years. Died on his birthday."

"We came to celebrate," Elsa whispered.

"That was your ancestor, Elsa. That Marstrand soldier."

"If you'd just written a line!"

Grandpop shut his eyes again on her, still partly bent on his planned death in his bed. His eyelids didn't move. His beard lay on the covers hiding his mouth that she knew was set as firm as hers had been last night prevailing against Bengt. Bengt had wanted Elsa to wait a week; by then Grandpop would have been gone.

She brought in the frozen milk to scald some in a pan in the kitchen. She crumbled the bread she had brought with her into a bowl and poured on the hot milk. She fed the old man, a napkin under his beard. He accepted it, his eyes hostile as those of the shot goose at home in the goat stable. Both man and bird held her guilty for halting them on their ways.

When the old man was done and sleeping in the warming room, Elsa put the children to sleep. Then she hunted Grandpop's clothes from the closets and drawers. She packed them into a crumbling false-leather portmanteau she found in an unused upstairs room where she had slept as a child visiting, where there was the odor of the lilacs that looked in whenever they bloomed. About were the remains of other lives, old wicker sewing baskets, needles still threaded, thrust into pincushions. A broken dish and a crushed vase on a little table told of carelessness or sudden wrath.

Bo woke roaring from his nap and Tina, unsettled, was squalling with him. Elsa hurried downstairs. She gave them bottles of the thawed milk to hush them, and then set them to playing with pots and pans from Grandmom's cupboard.

The old man roused a little and accepted the evening bread

The Goose

and milk she brought. He spooned some of it himself by the fluttering lamplight, shoving Elsa's hand from him with his own, gnarled, veined and dry. "Go away."

In the night, wakeful as over a child, Elsa went in to him. Petulant, he let her help him stagger from the bed to the bathroom and back. Her mind turned again on the wild goose, hungry and uneating, thirsty and undrinking, staring at her.

But in the morning he was almost gay, cackling to Bo when Elsa brought him coffee, "Your mama tell you how your ancestor got conscripted to fight against Napoleon! He trooped under Bernadotte, that Frenchy Carl Johann. They went as far as the Netherlands!"

He waved his arms in a new energy. Elsa wrapped a blanket about him and half-carried, half-led him to the Chevy. There she bundled him up in the back seat and put Tina on the floor in her basket beside the portmanteau. And they were off, back up into north Wisconsin. Grandpop slept most of the way. Bo beat time, patting his mittens together, and Elsa sang.

> *What a beautiful thought I am thinking,*
> *Concerning the great speckled bird,*
> *Remember her name is recorded*
> *On the pages of God's holy word!*

Grandpop started up when they were halfway home and mumbled a Swedish song Elsa finished for him, all about praise to the Lord Jesus, Herren Jesus.

"That's the Swedish blessing," Elsa told Bo, quiet, his small legs straight out before him, awed by the new family member throned in the back seat.

"She's right," said Grandpop. "And you pass that car ahead," he directed Elsa. "I always had the fastest buggy horse in town!" Then he fell asleep, his breathing as light as Tina's.

Bengt was astonished, and he and the hired man came tearing up from the corn when she pressed the horn. "Aa-aaa-roooo-

---

Children and Lovers

gah!" They left the team and wagon standing, the horses' noses down, nibbling at stray corn ears.

Bengt lifted Grandpop, rugs and all, and carried him to the poster bed in the guest room. The hand followed with Tina's basket and the portmanteau. And Elsa with the cake she'd made for Grandpop. Bo hustled in the rear.

"How's my wild goose, Bengt?" Elsa cried.

"There, Grandpop," Bengt said, pulling off Grandpop's boots and drawing the quilt up over him. "And welcome."

"How's my goose?"

"Such a question, wife!"

"I want to know."

He shrugged. "There. We've been busy and I forgot. But the hand milked out your goats last night and this morning. And we've got only one field of corn left to get in. This'll be a record year, I bet." He turned to Grandpop. "Filled the bins and had to build one new crib, old man."

As soon as Elsa could get away she was hurrying to the goat stable. The animals greeted her, pressing against her, licking the salt she brought them. The goose crouched against the farthest wall, silent. It staggered up as she came in, and hissed. The corn she had shelled for it was gone, and the water was ice-sheeted. She went to bring it a mash of ground cornmeal and hot water, and she set out fresh water.

The bird shied as she set its provisions down. It struck out at her with its wings and retreated, stretching its long neck up, its eyes watchful, the hiss ending in a honk.

"Hush, silly," she told it.

And as the days passed, the goose grew less afraid. After a while Elsa turned it in with the goats and it got on fine, even lying against them at night for warmth. One day it accepted corn from Bo's palm.

Grandpop healed along with the bird. On the same day it let Elsa and Bo stroke its dark back feathers, Grandpop was insist-

ing on breakfast in the kitchen with the rest of the family. He
said he was sick and tired of his early coffee and eggs alone in
his poster bed.

All that morning and in days thereafter, he sat in the rocker
in the kitchen window, where he could watch the men and the
shaggy fetlocked horses moving in the barnyard and far fields,
and the big black-and-white cows shuffling in their lot, and
Elsa's hens scratching about. And there was Bo strutting in his
heavy sweater and high boots, dragging his wagonful of the
wood horses Bengt and the hired man had carved and painted
for him.

And one day the wild goose came stalking in Bo's boot tracks,
weaving its thick neck, ingratiating, gabbling in a soft manner.
It tried to follow Bo up the porch stairs into the house and then
gave it up, and sat waiting for his return at the foot of the steps,
squatting in the snow.

Bo had refused his bottle, drinking now from a cup. After
he'd had his nap, he sat on the kitchen floor near Grandpop,
the milk cup before him, listening to long stories, fairy-tale and
true, about enchanted geese and Swedish wars with the rest of
the world and Bo's far-off relatives' heroic part in them.

Grandpop talked about old farming days in Wisconsin.
"When I was your age, my mama didn't give me goat milk in a
bottle like you were getting there a while back. She set me in
the cornshucks by the does and I got it straight from the teat!"

And Grandpop told of the lilac bush in town, reaching above
the highest windows. "One year you couldn't count the blooms
there were that many." And he spoke of a wild goose shot down
once in Grandmom's henyard. "The shot broke its leg and
wing. The wing healed straight, but it had a crooked leg."

Bo gazed, round-eyed, wanting to understand.

"It hopped," Grandpop cried, thumping on the floor with
the heavy hardwood cane Bengt had made him. "And then
every year the goose came back. Sometimes for a week, sometimes for the season. Old Crook-leg."

Children and Lovers

Bo went into the kitchen on one leg. "Old Crook-leg," he told Elsa. He went out to the goose, which followed him closely nowadays, sometimes consenting even to sitting in the wagon beside Bo's horses, and being hauled about by the sturdy child. "Old Crook-leg," he said to the goose and demonstrated.

Tina liked the old man too, and crawled on the sunwarm boards of the kitchen floor, grinning at him. She was learning to walk and pulled herself up at his knee beside the hardwood stick. She went staggering out into the room, losing her balance and sitting suddenly, remaining there a while, her thumb in her mouth.

Elsa took photographs to hang by the old ones. Bengt snapped one of all four of them, Tina on Grandpop's lap, Elsa behind, and Bo leaning on the arm of Grandpop's rocker, his leg crossed over, cocky.

Bengt asked a riddle, "What bird looks most like a goose, Bo?"

"Mrs. Goose," Bo said correctly and grinned, and Bengt pressed the shutter pin.

"Yay!" cried Elsa. And that was the snapshot she pinned on the wall.

And then spring began to come hesitantly to the northern state. Buds thought about bursting, and a wren pair arrived, ruffle-feathered, chilled, and chattered in the eaves. Bengt and the hired hand spent their hours walking in moist black furrows, ankle-deep in the loam, following the plowshares scoured shiny by the thawing earth.

Bo had his fourth birthday, and for the festivities, in a spring-windy day, Elsa took Grandpop's rocker out into the yard. He hobbled, relying on his cane in his right hand and Elsa at his left elbow to get him there safely. He settled himself, and she tucked blankets about his shoulders and around his knees. Then she went for the yellow cake with candles and a pitcher of fresh-drawn goat's milk and an armful of mugs to serve it in. She poured it for the guest and sliced the cake. Tina cooed at her feet.

Everyone came, even the wild goose, following Bo. Elsa had let the boy pull off his boots and socks, and Bo pattered ahead of the bird in the cold last-year's grass. The goose nibbled at his heels, and Bo squealed. Bengt was there and the hired man, their red shirts open, leaving the fields for two hours.

Crows called raucous, and a flock of bluebirds hid in a tree not far away. Bo's candles wouldn't stay lit. The wind struck them out. Bo sat on the old grass with the goose.

"In Sweden on this Island of Marstrand," Grandpop said, flourishing his cane, "there were snow-white swans. Every spring they came. Twice as big as that bird there. And long-necked, nothing like that goose!"

"According to you, old man," said Bengt, standing behind him, his hand on the withered shoulder, "everything in Sweden was twice the size or twice as good as in this new country."

"That's right," declared Grandpop, cackling.

Elsa had washed her hair and it hung in a loose damp coil. She cut the cake for seconds. "Want more, Birthday Boy?"

Bo's arm was around the goose, and it nibbled the sweet crumbs he held in his hand. "Have some, goose."

"Had to take a ferry to reach that island too. It's a fishing village and on the rock there's a castle," Grandpop said. "No new-fangled cars can get over there, even today." He waved his hand. "You'd have to fly them in."

When the party was over, the men returned to their plowing and Elsa to the kitchen with Tina. Bo and Grandpop remained. Bo lay on his back, the goose beside him, settled, preening. Grandpop's chin was sunk on his breast in his beard, his cane lay across his blanket-swathed knees. All three were half asleep when the wild geese began to come over, flying north to the next grounds.

There were three flocks streaming above in the sun-filled windy sky, and more arriving, dots in the distance. Their gabble was minor-keyed. "Quonk, onk," cried the leaders and the rear guards shouted back, "Onk!"

Idle, content, Bo and the old man turned their faces up to follow the bird flights. And then suddenly the bird at Bo's side had started up. It ran forward, its neck stretched, its button eyes brilliant, querying. It hissed, open-beaked in excitement, and spread its wings a little.

Bo sat up, startled. "Goose?"

"Let him alone," Grandpop whispered, his hand on his hardwood stick. "Let him be free."

The child sat still as the great bird gasped and then cried hoarsely up to its fellows, "Quonk!" It flapped its wings and stared.

When it began to run again, Bo was on his feet and after it. "No, goose!" As the bird spread its strong wings wide, Bo flung himself at it. "No!"

Alarmed, the bird turned upon its assailant, its sharp yellow beak digging at the restraining small arms. The heavy feathers scratched Bo's round cheeks, leaving red lines. The battle was uneven, and the goose should have won, but Bo was four now, and strong for his few years. And his desire was tremendous.

Grandpop cried, "Turn him loose now!"

But Bo pulled the wings together against the downy sides. He clasped them there, on his knees, his bare feet holding to the earth. "Grandpop. No."

The old man cast his blankets from his legs; he rose trembling, leaning on the big cane. "Let him go when I order you."

"Won't," the child squealed.

"Whoever had a more obstinate crowd of descendants!" With mouth as tight as Bo's he advanced. "I'll thrash you. Elsa's mama was disobedient in her marriage. You know that, boy! Are you going to be the same, standing against my wishes!"

Bo stared as the bird in his arms subsided, quiet, recognizing him. "Grandpop," Bo stammered. The weak figure, strengthened by anger, came towering now at him.

The Goose

And the old man was even quoting the Bible, yelling, "With-hold not correction from the child; for if thou beat him with the rod, he shall not die. Thou shalt beat him with the rod!"

As the cane descended, Bo rolled out of the way, the goose honking, but still tightly clasped to him. Then it fluttered free as Bo scrambled up and ran. The bird made no effort to fly now, but scuttled after Bo as they eluded their pursuer.

Grandpop's breath came in little gasps, hobbling, stumbling. "Catch you!"

But the pair were out of reach, leaving the yard, going down to the woods to hide, Bo crying back, "Hate you, Grandpop. Hate you!"

And his great-grandfather, his blue eyes watery and pale in wrath, almost sobbing, "Let that bird fly. I say!"

It was late in the afternoon when Bo crept up to the goat shed, the goose trailing after his bare feet. He'd spent the rest of the day watching the clamorous flocks pass over, leaning sullen against a tree bole, his arms around his pet. Now he shut the pen door on it, locking it in.

"Good night, goose," Bo told it. "And I'll never let you go."

He went up the porch steps and into the kitchen. Elsa said, "Wash your hands."

Bo, wary, splashed at the sink. "Where's Grandpop?"

"You have a nice day, four-year-old?" Elsa wanted to know.

"Where is he?" Bo shouted.

And Elsa looked at her small son, surprised, at his scratched face and legs. "Go put some shoes on. He's asleep. He had his bread and milk and says he's too tired for supper with us."

"Oh," said Bo and strutted from the room under her eyes. He felt his strength, his youth. He picked up his neglected wood horses, one at a time, and then hurled each back into the wagon. He walked about, restless, disturbed, uneasy. He thought it was because he feared his transformed Grandpop, once a gentle cackling teller of tales, and now become an ogre, shouting, swinging a great stick, face contorted.

In the morning Grandpop wasn't at the breakfast table. Elsa stood at the window, holding Tina, her back to the others. She said, "The geese are still flying today."

"This'll keep up for a week," Bengt said. "I bet. Day and night too."

"Where is he?" Bo got in his chair. He felt the strangeness, his mother's tense air. His voice was overloud.

"Tell him," Elsa said to Bengt.

"Grandpop died in his sleep," Bengt said.

Bo's eyes widened. "Grandpop."

"It was his time. He'd got past eighty where he wanted to be. He was ready."

"Where is he!" Bo got down from his chair.

He was running to the bedroom to catch the old man before he got farther away. He reached up for the knob and slammed the door against the wall as he hurled it open. Bo dashed to the bed and tugged the sheet from Grandpop's face.

Bengt waited in the doorway, ready for Bo's tears. "Easy, boy."

But Bo looked at Grandpop's impassive features, gentle again in sleep. He put a hand on the white beard. He frowned. "Papa. Grandpop chased me with a stick."

"Come away," Bengt said. "You be brave."

Bo felt Grandpop's hand, veined, and cold like the wild goose's web foot. He sighed and turned away, going past his father, asking, "What goes up but doesn't come down, Papa?"

"No time for riddles," Bengt said.

"My age," Bo said, clear voiced. He felt his immortality, a new wildness inside him.

As they watched the child stalk out of the kitchen and down the path outside, Bengt told Elsa, "He's brave. He never cried."

"I don't call that so brave." Elsa, again bereaved, put her face

---

The Goose

into Tina's neck for comfort. "And we'll get a fast funeral car too. Grandpop liked to pass all the cars up ahead."

Then from the open door in the distance, they saw the wild goose come fluttering, half-flying, out of the goat stable. He was followed by a changed Bo, fierce, waving his hands and shouting. They didn't hear his words:

"Turning him loose, Grandpop!"

"Why did he let it go?" Elsa turned to her husband, protesting. "And I thought he loved it so."

The goose ran on its web feet, peering into the sky where its fellows poured steadily. The great wings spread and rising, honking, it went to them, earth-freed. It merged with a flock, sweeping its wings in the old instinctive pattern, and following the line. It screamed its new elation in stretching the long-unused muscles, and also there was a tug of memory. The black button eyes glanced back at the earthling in the field far below, Bo, already beginning to wonder if the bird might return some day.

Children and Lovers